ALL YOU NEED IS
KILL

HIROSHI SAKURAZAKA

ALL YOU NEED IS KILL

HIROSHI SAKURAZAKA

TRANSLATED BY JOSEPH REEDER WITH
ALEXANDER O. SMITH

SAN FRANCISCO

HAIKASORU
Published by
VIZ Media, LLC
1355 Market Street, Suite 200
San Francisco, CA 94103

www.haikasoru.com

Sakurazaka, Hiroshi, 1970-
   [Oru yu nido izu kiru. English]
   All you need is kill / Hiroshi Sakurazaka; translated by Alexander O. Smith.
       p. cm.
   ISBN 978-1-4215-2761-1 (alk. paper)
   I. Smith, Alexander O. II. Title.
   PL875.5.A45O7813 2009
   895.6'36—dc22

                                                                2008051661

Printed in the U.S.A.
First printing, July 2009
Eighth printing, June 2021

CONTENTS

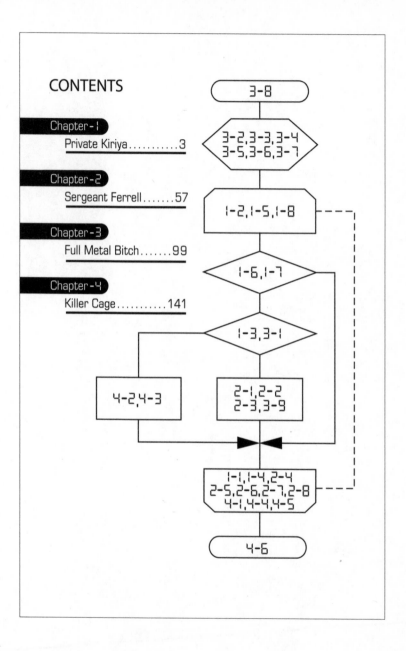

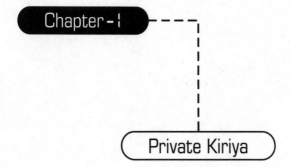

Chapter - 1

Private Kiriya

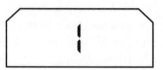

When the bullets start flying, it's only a matter of time before fear catches up with a soldier.

There you are, steel death whizzing past in the air.

Distant shells thunder low and muddy, a hollow sound you feel more than hear. The close ones ring high and clear. They scream with a voice that rattles your teeth, and you know they're the ones headed for you. They cut deep into the ground, throwing up a veil of dust that hangs there, waiting for the next round to come ripping through.

Thousands of shells, burning through the sky—slices of metal no bigger than your finger—and it only takes one to kill you. Only takes one to turn your best buddy into a steaming side of meat.

Death comes quick, in the beat of a heart, and he ain't picky about who he takes.

The soldiers he takes quick—before they know what hit 'em—they're the lucky ones. Most die in agony, their bones shattered, their organs shredded, leaking a sea of blood onto the ground. They wait alone in the mud for Death to steal up behind them and wring out the last drops of life with his icy hands.

If there's a heaven, it's a cold place. A dark place. A lonely place.

I'm terrified.

I grip the trigger with stiff fingers; my arms shake as I send a rain of scorching steel down onto the enemy. The rifle kicks as I fire it. *Vunk. Vunk. Vunk.* A beat steadier than my heart. A soldier's spirit isn't in his body. It's in his weapon. The barrel warms until it glows, the heat turning fear into anger.

Fuck the brass and their fucking pathetic excuse for air support!

Fuck the suits and their plans that aren't worth a damn once the shit starts flying!

Fuck the artillery for holding back on the left flank!

Fuck that bastard who just got himself killed!

And more than all of 'em, fuck anything and everything aiming at me! Wield your anger like a steel fist and smash in their faces.

If it moves, fuck it!

I have to kill them all. Stop them from moving.

A scream found its way through my clenched teeth.

My rifle fires 450 20mm rounds per minute, so it can burn through a clip fast. But there's no point holding back. It don't matter how much ammo you have left when you're dead. Time for a new magazine.

"Reload!"

The soldier I was shouting to was already dead. My order died in the air, a meaningless pulse of static. I squeezed my trigger again.

My buddy Yonabaru caught one of the first rounds they fired back—one of those javelins. Hit him straight on, tore right through his Jacket. The tip came out covered in blood, oil, and some unidentifiable fluids. His Jacket did a *danse macabre* for about ten seconds before it finally stopped moving.

There was no use calling a medic. He had a hole just below his chest nearly two centimeters across, and it went clean through his back. The friction had seared the wound at the edges, leaving a dull orange flame dancing around the opening. It all happened within the first minute after the order to attack.

He was the kind of guy that liked to pull rank on you over the stupidest shit, or tell you who'd done it in a whodunit before you'd finished the first chapter. But he didn't deserve to die.

My platoon—146 men from the 17th Company, 3rd Battalion, 12th Regiment, 301st Armored Infantry Division—was sent in to reinforce the northern end of Kotoiushi Island. They lifted us in by chopper to ambush the enemy's left flank from the rear. Our job was to wipe out the runners when the frontal assault inevitably started to push them back.

So much for inevitable.

Yonabaru died before the fighting even started.

I wondered if he suffered much.

By the time I realized what was going on, my platoon was smack dab in the middle of the battle. We were catching fire from the enemy and our own troops both. All I could hear were screams, sobbing, and "Fuck!" Fuck! Fuck! Fuck! The profanities were flying as thick as the bullets. Our squad leader was dead. Our sergeant was dead. The whir of the rotors on the support choppers was long gone. Comms were cut off. Our company had been torn to shreds.

The only reason I was still alive was because I'd been taking cover when Yonabaru bought it.

While the others stood their ground and fought, I was hiding in the shell of my Jacket, shaking like a leaf. These power suits are made of a Japanese composite armor plating that's the envy of the world. They cover you like white on rice. I figured that if a shell *did* make it past the first layer, it'd never make it past the second. So if I stayed out of sight long enough, the enemy would be gone when I came out. Right?

I was scared shitless.

Like any recruit fresh out of boot camp I could fire a rifle or a pile driver, but I still didn't know how to do it worth a damn. Anyone can squeeze a trigger. Bang! But knowing when to fire, where to shoot when you're surrounded? For the first time I realized I didn't know the first thing about warfare.

Another javelin streaked past my head.

I tasted blood in my mouth. The taste of iron. Proof that I was still alive.

My palms were clammy and slick inside my gloves. The vibrations of the Jacket told me the battery was almost out of juice. I smelled oil. The filter was on its last legs, and the stench of the battlefield was fighting its way into my suit, the smell of enemy corpses like the smell of crumpled leaves.

I hadn't felt anything below my waist for a while. It should have hurt where they hit me, but it didn't. I didn't know whether that was good or bad. Pain lets you know you're not dead yet. At least I didn't have to worry about the piss in my suit.

Out of fuel-air grenades. Only thirty-six 20mm slugs left. The magazine would be empty in five seconds. My rocket launcher—which they gave each of us only three rockets for anyway—got itself lost before I could even fire the damn thing. My head-mounted camera was wasted, the armor on my left arm was shredded, and even at full throttle the Jacket was only outputting at 40 percent. Miraculously, the pile driver on my left shoulder had survived without a scratch.

A pile driver is a close-combat weapon that uses an explosive charge to fire tungsten carbide spikes—only good against enemies within arm's reach. The powder cartridges it fires are each as big as a man's fist. At a ninety-degree angle of impact, the only thing that can stand up to it is the front armor plating on a tank. When they first told me its magazine only held twenty rounds, I didn't think anyone could live long enough to use even that many. I was wrong.

Mine had four rounds left.

I had fired sixteen times, and missed fifteen—maybe sixteen.

The heads-up display in my suit was warped. I couldn't see a goddamn thing where it was bent. There could be an enemy standing right in front of me and I'd never know it.

They say a vet who is used to the Jacket can get a read on his surroundings without even using the camera. Takes more than eyes in battle. You have to feel the impact passing through layers of ceramic and metal and into your body. Read the pull of the trigger. Feel the ground through the soles of your boots. Take in numbers from a kaleidoscope of gauges and know the state of the field in an instant. But I couldn't do any of that. A recruit in his first battle knows shit-all.

Breathe out. Breathe in.

My suit was rank with sweat. A terrible smell. Snot was seeping from my nose, but I couldn't wipe it.

I checked the chronometer beside my display. Sixty-one minutes had passed since the battle started. What a load of shit. It felt like I'd been fighting for months.

I looked left, right. Up, down. I made a fist inside one glove. Can't use too much strength, I had to remind myself. Overdo it, and my aim would drift low.

No time to check the Doppler. Time to fire and forget.

Thak thak thak thak thak!

A cloud of dust rose.

The enemy's rounds seemed to ride the wind over my head, but mine liked to veer off after leaving the barrel, as if the enemy simply willed them away. Our drill sergeant said guns could be funny like that. You ask me, it seems only fair that the enemy should get to hear shells screeching down on them, too. We should all have our turn feeling Death's breath on the back of our neck, friend and foe alike.

But what would Death's approach sound like to an inhuman enemy? Did they even feel fear?

Our enemies—the enemies of the United Defense Force—are monsters. Mimics, we call them.

My gun was out of bullets.

The silhouette of a misshapen orb materialized in the clay-brown haze. It was shorter than a man. It would probably come up to the shoulder of a Jacketed soldier. If a man were a thin pole standing on end, a Mimic would be a stout barrel—a barrel with four limbs and a tail, at any rate. Something like the bloated corpse of a drowned frog, we liked to say. To hear the lab rats tell it, they have more in common with starfish, but that's just details.

They make for a smaller target than a man, so naturally they're harder to hit. Despite their size, they weigh more than we do. If you took one of those oversized casks, the kind Americans use to distill bourbon, and filled it with wet sand you'd have it about right. Not the kind of mass a mammal that's 70 percent water could ever hope for. A single swipe of one of its limbs can send a man flying in a thousand little pieces. Their javelins, projectiles fired from vents in their bodies, have the power of 40mm shells.

To fight them, we use machines to make ourselves stronger. We climb into mechanized armor Jackets—science's latest and greatest. We bundle ourselves into steel porcupine skin so tough a shotgun fired at point blank wouldn't leave a scratch. That's how we face off against the Mimics, and we're still outclassed.

Mimics don't inspire the instinctive fear you'd expect if you found yourself facing a bear protecting her cubs, or meeting the gaze of a hungry lion. Mimics don't roar. They're not frightening to look at. They don't spread any wings or stand on their hind legs to make themselves look more intimidating. They simply hunt with the relentlessness of machines. I felt like a deer in the headlights, frozen in the path of an oncoming truck. I couldn't understand how I'd gotten myself into the situation I was in.

I was out of bullets.

So long, Mom.

I'm gonna die on a fucking battlefield. On some godforsaken island with no friends, no family, no girlfriend. In pain, in fear, covered in my own shit because of the fear. And I can't even raise the only weapon I have left to fend off the bastard racing toward me. It was like all the fire in me left with my last round of ammo.

The Mimic's coming for me.

I can hear Death breathing in my ear.

His figure looms large in my heads-up display.

Now I see him; his body is stained a bloody red. His scythe, a two-meter-long behemoth, is the same vivid shade. It's actually more of a battle axe than a scythe. In a world where friend and foe wear the same dust-colored camouflage, he casts a gunmetal red glow in all directions.

Death rushes forward, swifter than even a Mimic. A crimson leg kicks and I go flying.

My armor is crushed. I stop breathing. The sky becomes the ground. My display is drowning in red flashing warnings. I cough up blood, saving the rest of the warnings the trouble.

Then my pile driver fires. The blast throws me at least ten meters into the air. Bits of the armor plating from the back of my Jacket scatter across the ground. I land upside down.

Death swings his battle axe.

Metal screams as he cuts through the uncuttable. The axe cries out like a freight train screeching to a halt.

I see the Mimic's carapace sailing through the air.

It only took one blow to reduce the Mimic to a motionless heap. Ashen sand poured from the gaping wound. The two halves of the creature shuddered and twitched, each keeping its own strange rhythm. A creature humanity's greatest technological inventions could barely scratch, laid waste by a barbarian weapon from a thousand years past.

Death turned slowly to face me.

Amid the crush of red warning lights crowding my display, a sole green light winked on. An incoming friendly transmission. ". . . as a little . . . kay?" A woman's voice. Impossible to make it out over the noise. I couldn't stand. The Jacket was spent and so was I. It took everything I had left just to roll right side up.

Upon closer inspection, I was not, in fact, in the company of the Angel of Death. It was just another soldier in a Jacket. A Jacket not quite like my own, as it was outfitted with that massive battle axe where the regulation pile driver should have been. The insignia on the shoulder didn't read *JP* but instead *U.S.* In place of the usual desert camouflage mix of sand and coffee grounds, the suit shone head-to-toe in metallic crimson.

The Full Metal Bitch.

I'd heard stories. A war junkie always chasing the action, no matter where it led her. Word had it she and her Special Forces squad from the U.S. Army had chalked up half of all confirmed Mimic kills ever. Maybe anyone who could see that much fighting and live to tell about it really was the Angel of Death.

Still carrying the battle axe, the blazing red Jacket started toward me. Its hand reached down and fumbled for the jack in my shoulder plate. A contact comm.

"There's something I've been wantin' to know."

Her voice filled my suit, clear as crystal. A soft, light tone, at odds with the two-meter axe and carnage she'd just created with it.

"Is it true the green tea they serve in Japan at the end of your meal comes free?"

The conductive sand spilling out of the fallen Mimic danced away on the wind. I could hear the distant cry of shells as they flew. This was a battlefield, the scorched waste where Yonabaru, Captain Yuge, and the rest of my platoon had died. A forest of steel shells. A place where your suit fills with your own piss and shit. Where you drag yourself through a mire of blood and muck.

"I've gotten myself in trouble for believing everything I read. So I thought I'd play it safe, ask a local," she continued.

Here I am, half dead, covered in shit, and you want to talk about tea?

Who walks up to someone, kicks them to the ground, and then asks about tea? What was going through her fucking head? I wanted to give her a piece of my mind, but the words wouldn't come. I could think of the words I wanted to say, but my mouth had forgotten how to work—a litany of profanities stalled at the gate.

"That's the thing with books. Half the time the author doesn't know what the hell he's writing about—especially not those war novelists. Now how about you ease your finger off the trigger and take a nice, deep breath."

Good advice. It took a minute, but I started to see straight again. The sound of a woman's voice always had a way of calming me down. The pain I'd left in battle returned to my gut. My Jacket misread the cramps in my muscles, sending the suit into a mild spasm. I thought of the dance Yonabaru's suit did just before he died.

"Hurt much?"

"What do you think?" My reply wasn't much more than a hoarse whisper.

The red Jacket kneeled down in front of me, examining the shredded armor plate over my stomach. I ventured a question. "How's the battle going?"

"The 301st has been wiped out. Our main line fell back to the coast to regroup."

"What about your squad?"

"No use worrying about them."

"So . . . how do I look?"

"It pierced the front, but the back armor plate stopped it. It's charred bad."

"How bad?"

"Bad."

"Fuck me." I looked up at the sky. "Looks like it's starting to clear."

"Yeah. I like the sky here."

"Why's that?"

"It's clear. Can't beat islands for clear skies."

"Am I going to die?"

"Yeah," she told me.

I felt tears well up in my eyes. I was grateful then that the helmet hid my face from view. It kept my shame a private thing.

The red Jacket maneuvered to gently cradle my head. "What's your name? Not your rank or your serial number. Your name."

"Keiji. Keiji Kiriya."

"I'm Rita Vrataski. I'll stay with you until you die."

She couldn't have said anything I'd rather hear, but I wasn't going to let her see that. "You'll die too if you stay."

"I have a reason. When you die, Keiji, I'm going to take your Jacket's battery."

"That's cold."

"No need to fight it. Relax. Let go."

I heard an electronic squelch—an incoming comm signal in Rita's helmet. It was a man's voice. The link between our Jackets automatically relayed the voice to me.

"Calamity Dog, this is Chief Breeder."

"I read you." All business.

"Alpha Server and vicinity under control. Estimate we can hold for thirteen minutes, tops. Time to pick up that pizza."

"Calamity Dog copies. Running silent from here in."

The red Jacket stood, severing our comm link. Behind her an explosion rumbled. I felt the ground tremble through my spine. A laser-guided bomb had fallen from the sky. It plunged deep into the earth, piercing the bedrock before it detonated. The sandy white ground bulged like an overcooked pancake; its surface cracked and sent darker soil the color of maple syrup spewing into the air. A hail of mud splattered on my armor. Rita's battle axe glinted in the light.

The smoke cleared.

I could see a writhing mass in the center of the enormous crater left by the explosion: the enemy. Red points of light sprang to life on my radar screen, so many that every point was touching another.

I thought I saw Rita nod. She sprang forward, flitting across the battlefield. Her axe rose and fell. Each time it shone, the husk of a Mimic soared. The sand that poured from their wounds spiraled on the whirlwinds traced by her blade. She cut them down with the ease of a laser cutting butter. Her movements took her in a circle around me, protecting me. Rita and I had undergone the same training, but she was like a juggernaut while I lay on the ground, a stupid toy that had run down its batteries. No one had forced me to be here. I had dragged myself to this wasteland of a battlefield, and I wasn't doing a damn bit of good for anyone. Better I'd gotten plugged alongside Yonabaru. At least then I wouldn't have put another soldier in harm's way trying to protect me.

I decided not to die with three rounds left in my pile driver.

I lifted a leg. I put a hand on one knee.

I stood.

I screamed. I forced myself to keep going.

The red Jacket turned to me.

I heard some noise over my headphones, but I couldn't tell what she was trying to say.

One of the Mimics in the pack stood out from the rest. It wasn't that it looked different from the others. Just another drowned, bloated frog. But there was something about it that set it apart. Maybe proximity to death had sharpened my senses, but somehow I knew that was the one I was meant to fight.

So that's what I did. I leapt at the Mimic and it lashed out at me with its tail. I felt my body lighten. One of my arms had been cut off. The right arm—leaving the pile driver on the left intact. Lucky me. I pulled the trigger.

The charge fired, a perfect ninety-degree angle.

One more shot. A hole opened in the thing's carapace.

One more shot. I blacked out.

2

The paperback I'd been reading was beside my pillow.

It was a mystery novel about an American detective who is supposed to be some sort of expert on the Orient. I had my index finger wedged into a scene where all the key players meet for dinner at a Japanese restaurant in New York. The detective's client, an Italian, tries to order an espresso after their meal, but the detective stops him cold. He starts on about how at Japanese restaurants, they bring you green tea after dinner, so you don't have to order anything. Then he veers off on how green tea goes great with soy sauce, and oh, why is it that in India they spice their milk tea? He's finally gathered everyone involved in the case in one place, and he talks a blue streak about everything but who done it.

I rubbed my eyes.

Passing my hand over my shirt I felt my stomach through the cloth. I could make out a newly formed six-pack that hadn't been there half a year back. No trace of any wound, no charred flesh. My right arm was right where it should be. Good news all around. *What a crappy dream.*

I must have fallen asleep reading the book. I should have known something was up when Mad Wargarita started striking up small talk about mystery novels. American Special Operators who'd crossed the entire Pacific Ocean just for a taste of blood didn't have time to read the latest best seller. If they had spare time, they'd probably spend it tweaking their Jackets.

What a way to start the day. Today was going to be my first real taste of battle. Why couldn't I have dreamed about blasting away a few baddies, getting promoted a grade or two?

On the bunk above me a radio with its bass blown out was squawking music—some kind of prehistoric rock so ancient my old man wouldn't have recognized it. I could hear the sounds of the base stirring to life, incoherent chatter coming from every direction, and above it all, the DJ's over-caffeinated voice chirping away with the weather forecast. I could feel every word pierce my skull. Clear and sunny out here on the islands, same as yesterday, with a UV warning for the afternoon. *Watch out for those sunburns!*

The barracks weren't much more than four sheets of fire-resistant wood propped up together. A poster of a bronze-skinned bikini babe hung on one of the walls. Someone had replaced her head with a shot of the prime minister torn from the base newspaper. The bikini babe's head grinned vapidly from its new home atop a macho muscle builder on another nearby poster. The muscle builder's head was MIA.

I stretched in my bunk. The welded aluminum frame squealed in protest.

"Keiji, sign this." Yonabaru craned his neck over the side of the top bunk. He looked great for a guy I'd just seen get impaled. They say people who die in dreams are supposed to live forever.

Jin Yonabaru had joined up three years before me. Three more years of trimming the fat, three more years of packing on muscle. Back when he was a civilian he'd been thin as a beanpole. Now he was cut from rock. He was a soldier, and he looked the part.

"What is it?"

"A confession. The one I told you about."

"I signed it yesterday."

"Really? That's weird." I could hear him rifling through pages above me. "No, not here. Well, sign one for me again, will ya?"

"You trying to pull a fast one on me?"

"Only if you come back in a bodybag. Besides, you can only die once, so what difference does it make how many copies you sign?"

UDF soldiers on the front line had a tradition. The day before an operation, they'd sneak into the PX and make off with some liquor. Drink and be merry, for tomorrow we die. The shot they gave you before battle broke down any acetaldehyde left in the bloodstream. But if you were caught, they'd bring you up before a disciplinary committee—maybe a court martial if you screwed the pooch real bad—after taking stock of inventory once the fighting was over and everyone was back on base. Of course, it was hard to court-martial a corpse. Which is why we'd all leave notes before the battle explaining how the robbery had been our idea. Sure enough, when the investigation started, it was always some poor sap who'd got himself killed who had masterminded the whole thing. It was a good system. The people running the PX were wise to the racket, so they made sure to leave out some bottles that wouldn't be missed too much. You'd think they'd just go ahead and give everyone a few drinks the night before a battle—for morale's sake, if nothing else—but no, it was the same old song and dance every time. Good ideas don't stand a chance against good bureaucracy.

I took the paper from Yonabaru. "Funny, I thought I'd be more nervous."

"So soon? Save it for the day, man."

"What do you mean? We suit up this afternoon."

"You nuts? How long you plan on wearing that thing?"

"If I don't wear it today, when will I?"

"How about tomorrow, when we roll out?"

I nearly fell out of bed. For an instant, my eyes settled on the soldier lying on the bunk next to mine. He was flipping through a porn magazine. Then I stared up into Yonabaru's face.

"What do you mean, tomorrow? They postpone the attack?"

"No, man. It's always been tomorrow. But our secret mission to get hammered starts tonight at nineteen hundred hours. We drink ourselves blind and wake up with a helluva hangover in the morning. A plan not even HQ could fuck up."

Wait. We'd broken into the PX last night. I remembered the whole thing. I was nervous about it being my first battle, so I'd decided to duck out a bit early. I had come back to my bunk and started reading that mystery novel. I even remembered helping Yonabaru up to his bed when he came staggering in from partying with the ladies.

Unless—unless I had dreamed that too?

Yonabaru smirked. "You don't look so good, Keiji."

I picked the novel up off my bed. I'd brought it along to read in my spare time, but I'd been so busy drilling formation that it had stayed stuffed in the bottom of my bag. I remember thinking how appropriately ironic it was that I hadn't had any time to start reading it until the day before I was probably going to die. I opened the book to the last page I'd read. The American detective who was supposed to be an expert on the Orient was discussing the finer points of green tea, just like I remembered. If today was the day before the battle, when had I read the book? Nothing was making any sense.

"Listen. There's nothin' to tomorrow's operation."

I blinked. "Nothin' to it, huh?"

"Just get yourself home without shooting anyone in the back, and you'll be fine."

I grunted in reply.

Yonabaru curled his hand into a gun and pointed his index finger at his head. "I'm serious. Sweat it too much, you'll turn into a feedhead—end up losing your mind before they even get a chance to blow your brains out."

The guy I'd replaced had gone a little haywire, so they pulled him from the front lines. They say he started picking up comm feeds about how humanity was doomed. Not the kind of shit you want heavily armed UDF Jacket jockeys listening to. We might not lose as many to that as we do to the enemy, but it's not pretty either way. In battle, unless you're sound of body and mind, you're a liability. I'd only just arrived on the front lines—hadn't even seen any action—and already I was having hallucinations. Who knows what warning lights were going off in my head.

"You ask me, anyone come out of battle not actin' a little funny has a screw or three loose." Yonabaru grinned.

"Hey, no scarin' the fresh meat," I protested. I wasn't actually scared, but I was growing increasingly confused.

"Just look at Ferrell! Only way to make it is to lose whatever it is that makes you human. A sensitive, caring indiv'dual like myself ain't cut out for fightin', and that's the truth."

"I don't see anything wrong with the sergeant."

"Ain't a question of right or wrong. It's about having a heart made of tungsten and muscles so big they cut off the blood to your brain."

"I wouldn't go that far."

"Next you'll be tellin' us that Mad Wargarita is just another grunt like the rest of us."

"Yeah, well, the thing with her is—" and so the conversation went on, back and forth like we always did. Our badmouthing of Rita was just hitting its stride when the sergeant showed up.

Sergeant Bartolome Ferrell had been around longer than anyone else in our platoon. He'd lived through so many battles, he was more than soldier, he was the glue that kept our company together. They said if you stuck him in a centrifuge, he'd come out 70 percent big brother, 20 percent ball-busting drill sergeant, and 10 percent steel-reinforced carbon. He scowled at me, then looked at Yonabaru, who was hastily bundling up our liquor confessions. His scowl deepened. "You the soldier who broke into the PX?"

"Yeah, that's me," my friend confessed without a trace of guilt.

The men on the surrounding beds ducked under their sheets with all the speed of cockroaches scattering in the light, porn magazines and playing cards forgotten. They'd seen the look on the sergeant's face.

I cleared my throat. "Did security, uh . . . run into some kind of trouble?"

Ferrell's forehead knotted as though he were balancing a stack of armored plating on his head. I had a strong feeling of déjà vu. *All this happened in my dream!* Something had gone down, unrelated, at the exact time Yonabaru and his buddies were breaking into the PX. Security had gone on alert, and the robbery had come to light ahead of schedule. "Where'd you hear that?"

"Just, uh, a lucky guess."

Yonabaru leaned out over the edge of his bunk. "What kind of trouble?"

"Someone stepped in a knee-deep pile of pig shit. Now that may not have anything to do with you, but nevertheless, at oh-nine-hundred, you're going to assemble at the No. 1 Training Field in your fourth-tier equipment for Physical Training. Pass the word to the rest of those knuckleheads you call a platoon."

"You gotta be kidding! We're goin' into battle tomorrow, and you're sending us off for PT?"

"That's an order, Corporal."

"Sir, reporting to the No. 1 Training Field at oh-nine-hundred in full fourth-tier equipment, sir! But, uh, one thing, Sarge. We been doin' that liquor raid for years. Why give us a hard time about it now?"

"You really want to know?" Ferrell rolled his eyes. I swallowed hard.

"Nah, I already know the answer." Yonabaru grinned. He always seemed to be grinning. "It's because the chain of command around here is fucked to hell."

"You'll find out for yourself."

"Wait, Sarge!"

Ferrell took three regulation-length paces and stopped.

"C'mon, not even a hint?" Yonabaru called from where he was taking cover behind the metal bed frame and bundled confessions.

"The general's the one with his panties in a bunch about the rotten excuse for security we have on this base, so don't look at me, and don't look at the captain, either. In fact, you might as well just shut up and do what you're told for a change."

I sighed. "He's not gonna have us out there weaving baskets, is he?"

Yonabaru shook his head. "Maybe we can all do a group hug. Fucking asshole."

I knew where this ended. I'd dreamed all this, too.

After their defeat a year and a half ago at the Battle of Okinawa Beach, the Japanese Corps made it a matter of honor to recapture a little island perched off the coast of the Boso Peninsula, a place named Kotoiushi. With a foothold there, the Mimics were only a stone's throw away from Tokyo. The Imperial Palace and central government retreated and ruled from Nagano, but there wasn't any way to relocate the economic engine that was Japan's largest city.

The Defense Ministry knew that Japan's future was riding on the outcome of this operation, so in addition to mustering twenty-five thousand Jackets, an endless stream of overeager generals had been pooling in this little base on the Flower Line that led down the Boso Peninsula. They'd even decided to allow Americans, Special Operators, into the game; the U.S. hadn't been invited to the party at Okinawa.

The Americans probably didn't give a damn whether or not Tokyo was reduced to a smoking wasteland, but letting the industrial area responsible for producing the lightest, toughest composite armor plating fall to the Mimics was out of the question. Seventy percent of the parts that went into a state-of-the-art Jacket came from China, but the suits still couldn't be made without Japanese technology. So convincing the Americans to come hadn't been difficult.

The catch was that with foreign troops came tighter security. Suddenly there were checks on things like missing alcohol that base security would have turned a blind eye to before. When the brass found out what had been going on, they were royally pissed.

"How's that for luck? I wonder who fucked up."

"It ain't us. I knew the Americans would be watchin' over their precious battalion like hawks. We were careful as a virgin on prom night."

Yonabaru let out an exaggerated moan. "Ungh, my stomach . . . Sarge! My stomach just started hurtin' real bad! I think it's my appendix. Or maybe I got tetanus back when I hurt myself training. Yeah, that's gotta be it!"

"I doubt it will clear up before tonight, so just make sure you stay hydrated. It won't last until tomorrow, hear me?"

"Oh, man. It really hurts."

"Kiriya. See that he drinks some water."

"Sir."

Ignoring Yonabaru's continued performance, Ferrell walked out of the barracks. As soon as his audience was gone, Yonabaru sat up and made a rude gesture in the direction of the door. "He's really got a stick up his ass. Wouldn't understand a good joke if it came with a fucking manual. Ain't no way I'm gonna be like that when I get old. Am I right?"

"I guess."

"Fuck, fuck, fuck. Today is turnin' to shit."

It was all playing out how I remembered.

The 17th Armored would spend the next three hours in PT. Exhausted, we would listen to some commissioned officer, his chest bristling with medals, lecture us for another half hour before being dismissed. I could still hear him threatening to pluck the hairs off our asses one by one with Jacket-augmented fingers.

My dream was looking less like one by the minute.

3

There's an exercise called an iso push-up. You lift your body like you would in an ordinary push-up, then you hold that position.

It's a lot harder than it sounds. You can feel your arms and abs trembling, and eventually you lose your sense of time. After you've counted something like the thousandth sheep jumping a fence, you'll beg to be doing ordinary push-ups, anything but this. Your arms aren't designed to be pillars. Muscles and joints are there to flex and bend. Flex and bend. Sounds nice just thinking about it. But you can't think about it, or you'll feel even worse. *You're pillars, hear me? Pillars! Nice strong pillars.*

Muscle isn't really all that important for a Jacket jockey. Whether a person's grip is thirty kilos or seventy, as soon as they put on that Jacket, they'll have 370 kilos of force in the palm of their hands. What a Jacket jockey needs is endurance and control—the ability to hold one position without twitching a muscle.

Iso push-ups are just the thing for that. Wall sitting isn't half bad, either.

Some claimed iso push-ups had become the favored form of discipline in the old Japan Self-Defense Force after they banned corporal punishment. I had a hard time believing the practice had survived long enough to be picked up by the Armored Infantry Division—the JSDF had joined the UDF before I was even born. But whoever thought of it, I hope he died a slow, painful death.

"Ninety-eight!"
"NINETY-EIGHT!" we all cried out.
"Ninety-nine!"
"NINETY-NINE!"
Staring into the ground, we barked desperately in time with the drill sergeant, sweat streaming into our eyes.
"Eight hundred!"
"EIGHT HUNDRED!"
Fuck OFF!
Our shadows were crisp and clear under the scorching sun. The company's flag snapped and fluttered high above the field. The wind that buffeted the training grounds reeked of salt and left a briny layer of slime on our skin.

There, motionless in the middle of that gargantuan training field, 141 men from the 17th Company of the Armored Infantry Division held their iso push-ups. Three platoon leaders stood, as motionless as their men, one in front of each platoon. Our captain watched over the scene with a grimace from the shade of the barracks tent. Sitting beside him was a brigadier general from the General Staff Office. The general who'd opened his mouth and started this farce was probably off sipping green tea in an air-conditioned office. *Cocksucker.*

A general was a being from the heavens above. A being perched on a gilded throne, higher than me, higher than Yonabaru, higher than Ferrell, higher than the lieutenant in charge of our platoon, the captain in charge of our company, the lieutenant colonel in charge of our battalion; higher than the colonel in charge of our regiment, higher even than the base commander. The generals were the gods of Flower Line and all who trained, slept, and shat within its walls. So high, they seemed distant and unreal.

Generals didn't steal liquor. They were early to bed, early to rise, always brushing their teeth after every meal, never skipping a morning shave—goddamned messiahs. Generals went into battle facing death with their chins held high, calm as you please. Hell, all they had to do was sit back in Nagano drawing up their battle plans. One order from them and us mortals on the front lines would move like pawns across a chessboard to our grisly fates. I'd like to see just one of them here with us in the mud. We had our own rules down here. Which is probably why they stayed away. Hell, if one of them showed, I'd see to it a stray bullet put them on the KIA list. This was the least damning thought running through my head, any one of which would have been enough to send me to a firing squad.

The brass in the tent weren't the only spectators around to watch our torture.

The guys in 4th Company were really laughing it up. A while back we beat them in an intramural rugby match by more than thirty points, so I guess they felt this was some sort of twisted payback. The liquor we'd swiped was for them too, so this display of solidarity was touching. What a bunch of assholes. If they got into trouble on Kotoiushi, I sure as hell wasn't going to bail them out.

The U.S. Spec Ops and some journalist embedded in their squad had gathered around the field to watch us from a safe distance. Maybe they didn't do iso push-ups where they came from, but whatever the reason, they were pointing their fat fingers at us and laughing. The breeze coming off the water picked up their voices and dumped them on us. Even at this distance, the commentary was loud and grating. Fingernails on a chalkboard grating. Oh, man. Is that a camera? Is he seriously taking pictures? All right, that's it, motherfucker. You're next on my KIA list.

Pain and fatigue racked my body. My blood pumped slow as lead.

This was getting old. Counting my dream, this was the second time I'd endured this particular session of PT. Not just PT, iso push-ups. In training they taught us that even when you're in excruciating pain—*especially* when you're in pain—the best thing to do was to find some sort of distraction, something else to focus on other than the burning in your muscles and the sweat streaking down your forehead. Careful not to move my head, I looked around out of the corner of one eye.

The American journalist was snapping pictures, a visitor's pass dangling from his neck. *Say cheese!* He was a brawny fellow. You could line him up with any of those U.S. Special Forces guys and you'd never know the difference. He'd look more at home on a battlefield than I would, that's for sure.

I got the same vibe from those Special Forces guys that I got from Sergeant Ferrell. Pain and suffering were old friends to men like them. They walked up to the face of danger, smiled, and asked what took him so long to get there. They were in a whole 'nother league from a recruit like me.

In the middle of the testosterone display, the lone woman stuck out like a sore pinky. She was a tiny little thing standing off by herself a short distance from the rest of the squad. Seeing her there beside the rest of her super-sized squad, something seemed out of whack.

Anne of Green Gables Goes to War.

I figure the book would be a spin-off set around World War I. Mongolia makes a land grab, and there's Anne, machine gun tucked daintily under one arm. Her hair was the color of rusted steel, faded to a dull red. Some redheads conjured up images of blood, fire, deeds of valor. Not her. If it weren't for the sand-colored shirt she was wearing, she'd have looked like some kid who'd come to the base on a field trip and gotten herself lost.

The others were fanned out around this girl who barely came up to their chests like awed, medieval peasants gawking at nobility.

Suddenly it hit me. *That's Rita!*

It had to be. It was the only way to explain how this woman, who couldn't have looked less like a Jacket jockey if she had been wearing a ball gown, was in the company of the spec ops. Most women who suited up looked like some sort of cross between a gorilla and an uglier gorilla. They were the only ones who could cut it on the front lines in the Armored Infantry.

Rita Vrataski was the most famous soldier in the world. Back when I signed up for the UDF, you couldn't go a day without seeing the news feeds sing her praises. Stories titled "A Legendary Commando," "Valkyrie Incarnate," that sort of thing. I'd even heard Hollywood was gonna make a movie about her, but I was already in the UDF by the time it came out, so I never saw it.

About half of all the Mimic kills humanity had ever made could be attributed to battles her squad had fought in. In less than three years, they'd slaughtered as many Mimics as the whole UDF put together had in the twenty years before. Rita was a savior descended from on high to help turn the odds in this endless, losing battle.

That's what they said, anyway.

We all figured she was part of some propaganda squad they were using to make inroads into enemy territory. A front for some secret weapon or new strategy that really deserved the credit. Sixty percent of soldiers were men. That figure shot up to 85 percent when you started talking about the Jacket jockeys who were out bleeding on the front lines. After twenty years fighting an enemy whose identity we didn't even know, losing ground day by day, we grunts didn't need another muscle-bound savior who grunted and sweat and had hamburger for brains just like we did. Yeah, if it were me calling the shots in the General Staff Office, I'd have picked a woman too.

Wherever the U.S. Spec Ops were deployed, morale soared. The UDF had been beaten to the cliff's edge, but they were finally able to start moving back from the brink. After finishing the war in North America, they moved on to Europe and then North Africa. Now they'd come to Japan, where the enemy was knocking on the door of the main island of Honshu.

The Americans called Rita the Full Metal Bitch, or sometimes just Queen Bitch. When no one was listening, we called her Mad Wargarita.

Rita's Jacket was as red as the rising sun. She thumbed her nose at the lab coats who'd spent sleepless months refining the Jackets' polymer paint to absorb every last radar wave possible. Her suit was gunmetal red—no, more than that, it glowed. In the dark it would catch the faintest light, smoldering crimson. Was she crazy? Probably.

Behind her back they said she painted her suit with the blood of her squad. When you stand out like that on the battlefield, you tend to draw more than your share of enemy fire. Others said she'd stop at nothing to make her squad look good, that she even took cover behind a fellow soldier once. If she had a bad headache, she'd go apeshit, killing friend and foe alike. And yet not a single enemy round had ever so much as grazed her Jacket. She could walk into any hell and come back unscathed. They had a million stories.

Your rank and file soldier ended up with a lot of time on his hands, and listening to that sort of talk, passing it on, embellishing it—that was just the sort of thing he needed to kill time and to keep the subject off dead comrades. Rita had been a Jacket jockey eating and sleeping on the same base as me, but I'd never seen her face until that moment. We might have resented the special treatment she got, if we'd had the chance to think about it.

I couldn't take my eyes off the line of her hair—she wore it short—as it bobbed in the wind. There was a graceful balance to her features. You might even have called her beautiful. She had a thin nose, a sharp chin. Her neck was long and white where most Jacket jockeys didn't even have necks. Her chest, however, was completely flat, at odds with the images of Caucasian women you saw plastered on the walls of every barracks cell. Not that it bothered me.

Whoever had looked at her and thought up the name Full Metal Bitch needed to have his head checked. She was closer to a puppy than a bitch. I suppose even in a litter of pit bulls there's room for one sweet one in the bunch.

If, in my dream, the shell of that red Jacket had popped open and she'd climbed out, I would have shit my bunk. I'd seen her face and Jacket plenty on the news feeds, but they never gave you a good idea of what she really looked like in person. I had always pictured Rita Vrataski as tall and ruthless, with a knockout body and an air of total self-confidence.

Then our eyes met.

I looked away immediately, but it was already too late. She started walking toward me. She moved with purpose, one foot planted firmly on the ground before the other moved—a relentless, unstoppable force. But her steps were small, the net result being a harried, flustered gait. I'm not sure I'd ever seen anyone walk quite like that before.

C'mon, don't do this to me. I can't even move. Give a guy a break and get lost, would ya? Go on. Get!

Rita stopped.

The muscles in my arms started to tremble. Then, purposefully, she walked away. Somehow she'd heard my prayer, making a ninety-degree turn right in front of me and heading toward the brigadier general where he sat under the tent. She snapped a perfunctory salute. Not so sloppy as to be insulting, but not so stiff you could hear anything cracking, either. A fitting salute for the Full Metal Bitch.

The brigadier general cast a doubtful glance at Rita. Rita was a sergeant major. In the military hierarchy, the difference between a brigadier general and a sergeant major was about the same as the difference between a four-course meal at a snooty restaurant and an all-you-can-eat buffet. Recruits like me were strictly fast food, complete with an oversized side of fries. But it wasn't that simple. It never was. Rita was U.S. military, the linchpin of the upcoming operation, and one of the most important soldiers on the face of the planet. Rank aside, it was hard to say which one of them really held more power.

Rita stood in silence. The brigadier general was the first to speak.

"Yes, Sergeant?"

"Sir, would it be possible for me to join the PT, sir."

The same high voice from my dream, speaking in perfectly intoned Burst.

"You have a major operation coming up tomorrow."

"So do they, sir. My squad has never participated in this form of PT, sir. I believe my participation could be vital in ensuring the successful coordination and execution of tomorrow's joint operation."

The general was at a loss for words. The U.S. Special Forces around the field started to whoop and cheer.

"Request permission to participate in the PT, sir," she said.

"Granted."

"Sir, thank you, sir!"

She flashed a quick salute. Doing an about-face, she slipped among the rows of men staring intently into the ground.

She chose a spot beside me and started her iso push-up. I could feel the heat coming off her body through the chilly air between us.

I didn't move. Rita didn't move. The sun hung high in the sky, showering its rays over us, slowly roasting our skin. A drop of sweat formed in my armpit, then traced its way slowly to the ground. Sweat had started to bead on Rita's skin too. Fuck! I felt like a chicken crammed into the same oven as the Christmas turkey.

Rita's lips made the subtlest of movements. A low voice only I could hear.

"Do I have something on my face?"

"What?"

"You've been staring at me for a while now."

"Me? No."

"I thought maybe there was a laser bead on my forehead."

"Sorry. There wasn't—it's nothing."

"Oh. All right."

"Shit-for-brains Kiriya! You're slipping!" the lieutenant barked. I quickly extended my arm back into position. Beside me, Rita Vrataski, with the disinterested expression of someone who'd never had a need for human contact her entire life, continued her iso push-up.

PT ended less than an hour later. The general, the taste of bile in his mouth forgotten, returned to the barracks without further instructions. The 17th Company had spent a productive pre-battle afternoon.

It hadn't played out the way I remembered it. In my dream, I never made eye contact with Rita, and she hadn't joined in the PT. Maybe I was reading too much into things, but I'd say she did it just to piss the general off. It took a Valkyrie reborn to throw a monkey wrench into a disciplinary training session planned with military precision and get away with it. Then again, her antenna may just have picked up something that made her want to see what this weird iso push-up thing was all about. Maybe she had just been curious.

One thing was for sure, though. Rita Vrataski wasn't the bitch everyone made her out to be.

4

"How about last night, huh? That shit was tight."

"You said it."

"With reflexes like that, that girl must be hiding springs in that little body of hers. I could feel it all the way into my abs."

"She hears you talkin' like that, best watch out."

"Who doesn't like a compliment? I'm just sayin' she was good." As he spoke, Yonabaru thrust his hips.

Seeing someone move like that in a Jacket was pretty damn funny. An everyday gesture with enough power behind it to level a house.

Our platoon was on the northern tip of Kotoiushi Island, waiting to spring the ambush, Jackets in sleep mode. A screen about half a meter tall stood in front of us, projecting an image of the terrain behind. It's what they called active camouflage. It was supposed to render us undetectable from an enemy looking at us head on. Of course, we could have just used a painting. The terrain had been bombed into oblivion, so any direction you looked, all you saw was the same charred wasteland.

Most of the time, the Mimics lurked in caves that twisted deep under the seabed. Before a ground assault, we fired bunker buster bombs that penetrated into the ground before detonating. *Eat that.* Each one of those babies cost more than I'd make in my entire lifetime. But the Mimics had an uncanny way of avoiding the bombs. It was enough to make you wonder if they were getting a copy of our attack plans in advance. On paper we may have had air superiority, but we ended up in a drawn-out land war anyhow.

Since our platoon was part of an ambush, we weren't packing the large-bore cannons—massive weapons that were each the size of a small car fully assembled. What we did have were 20mm rifles, fuel-air grenades, pile drivers, and rocket launchers loaded with three rounds apiece. Since it was Ferrell's platoon, we were all linked to him via comm. I glanced at my Jacket's HUD. It was twenty-eight degrees Celsius. Pressure was 1014 millibars. The primary strike force would be on the move any minute.

Last night, after that endless hour of PT, I'd decided to go to the party. It wasn't what I remembered doing from the dream, but I didn't really feel like rereading that book. The part about helping Yonabaru up to his bunk after he stumbled back to the barracks stayed the same.

Word around the platoon was that Yonabaru's girlfriend was a Jacket jockey too. With the exception of Special Forces, men and women fought in separate platoons, so we wouldn't have run into her on the battlefield anyway.

"If—and I'm just talkin'—but if one of you got killed . . ." I ventured.

"I'd feel like shit."

"But you still see each other anyway."

"Heaven ain't some Swiss bank. You can't squirrel away money in some secret account up there and expect to make a withdrawal. You gotta do what you can before goin' into battle. That's the first rule of soldierin'."

"Yeah, I guess."

"But I'm tellin' ya, you gotta hook yourself up with some pussy. Carpe diem, brother."

"Carpe something."

"What about Mad Wargarita? Y'all were talkin' during PT, right? You'd tap that, I know you would."

"Don't even go there."

"Tiny girl like her—I bet she's a wolverine in the sack. The smaller they are, the better they fuck, you know."

"Show some respect."

"Sex ain't got nothin' to do with respect. From the lowest peon to His Majesty the general, everybody wants to do a little poundin' between the legs. All I'm sayin' is that's how we evolved—"

"Just shut the fuck up," I said.

"That any way to talk to me in front of the sergeant? I'm hurt. I've got a very sensitive disposition. I'm just talkin' trash to keep my mind off things. Same as everybody else."

"He's right," someone else chipped in over the comm link.

"Hey, don't I get a vote?"

It was like this was the excuse everyone in the platoon had been waiting for. Everyone started talking at once.

"I'm gonna have to cast my ballot for Yonabaru."

"I've set this thing to filter out your jokes, so stop wastin' your breath."

"Sounds like Kiriya's gonna have to step up his training if he doesn't want Yonabaru to take the piss out of him so easy."

"Sir! I think I need to reboot my Jacket, sir! I don't want it crashing during the battle!"

"Aw man, I'd kill for a cigarette. Musta left 'em in my other Jacket."

"I thought you quit smokin'?"

"Hey, keep it down! I'm tryin' to get some sleep!"

And so it went. Back and forth through the comm link, like it was an Internet chat room. All Ferrell could do was sigh and shake his Jacketed head.

When you're so nervous you've run out of nails to bite, thinking about something you enjoy helps take the pressure off. They taught us that in training too. Of course, you get a bunch of animals like these together, pretty much the only thing they think about is sex. There was only one girl I could think about, my sweet little librarian whose face I could hardly picture anymore. Who knew what she was doing. It'd been half a year since she got married. She was probably knocked up by now. I enlisted right after I graduated from high school, and she broke my heart. I don't think the two things were related. Who can say?

I had signed up thinking I could make some sense of this fucked-up world by betting my life in battle and seeing what fate dealt me. Boy was I ever green. If I was tea-green now, I must've been lime-green back then. Turns out my life isn't even worth enough to buy one of those pricey bombs, and what cards fate has dealt me don't have any rhyme or reason.

"Nuts to this. If we're not gonna dig trenches, can't we at least sit?"

"Can't hide if we're diggin' trenches."

"This active camouflage ain't good for shit. Who's to say they don't see better'n we do, anyhow? They aren't supposed to be able to see the attack choppers either, but they knock 'em out of the sky like balloons in a shootin' gallery. Made for a helluva time at Okinawa."

"If we run into the enemy, I'll be sure to give 'em an eye test."

"I still say the trench is man's greatest invention. My kingdom for a trench."

"You can dig all the trenches you want once we get back. My orders."

"Isn't that how they torture prisoners?"

"My pension to the man who invents a way to fasten your—shit, it's started! Don't get your balls blown off, gents!" Ferrell shouted.

The din of battle filled the air. I could feel the shudder of distant shells exploding.

I turned my attention to Yonabaru. After what happened in PT, maybe my dream was just a dream, but if Yonabaru died by my side at the beginning of the battle, I'd never forgive myself. I replayed the events of the dream in my head. The javelin had come from two o'clock. It had flown right through the camouflage screen, leaving it in tatters, all about a minute after the battle started, give or take.

I tensed my body, ready to be knocked down at any moment.

My arms were shaking. An itch developed in the small of my back. A wrinkle in my inner suit pressed against my side.

What are they waiting for?

The first round didn't hit Yonabaru.

The shot that was supposed to have killed him was headed for me instead. I didn't have time to move a millimeter. I'll never forget the sight of that enemy javelin flying straight at me.

5

The paperback I'd been reading was beside my pillow.

It was a mystery novel about an American detective who was supposed to be some sort of expert on the Orient. I had my index finger wedged into a scene where all the key players meet for dinner at a Japanese restaurant in New York.

Without rising, I looked carefully around the barracks. Nothing had changed. The swimsuit pinup still had the prime minister's head. The radio with the busted bass grated out music from the top bunk; from beyond the grave a singer admonished us against crying over a lost love. After waiting to be sure the DJ would read the weather report in her bubblegum voice, I sat up.

I shifted my weight as I sat on the edge of the bed.

I pinched my arm as hard as I could. The spot I pinched started to turn red. It hurt like a bitch. Tears blurred my vision.

"Keiji, sign this."

Yonabaru craned his neck over the side of the top bunk.

". . ."

"What's the matter? Still asleep?"

"Nah. You need my signature? Sure."

Yonabaru disappeared from view.

"Mind if I ask something a little weird?"

"What? I just need you to sign on the dotted line." His voice came from over the bed frame. "Don't need you to write anything else. No funny drawings of the lieutenant on the back or nothin'."

"Why would I do that?"

"I dunno. It's what I did the first time I signed."

"Don't start comparing—ah, forget it. What I wanted to ask was, the attack's tomorrow, right?"

"Sure. That's not the kinda thing they go changin' up."

"You've never heard of anyone reliving the same day over and over, have you?"

There was a pause before he replied. "You sure you're awake? The day after yesterday's today. The day after today is tomorrow. If it didn't work like that, we'd never get to Christmas or Valentine's Day. Then we'd be fucked. Or not."

"Yeah. Right."

"Listen. There's nothin' to tomorrow's operation."

". . . Right."

"Sweat it too much, you'll turn into a feedhead—end up losing your mind before they even get a chance to blow your brains out."

I stared blankly at the aluminum piping of the bed frame.

When I was a kid, the war against the Mimics had already started. Instead of cowboys and Indians or cops and robbers, we fought aliens using toy guns that fired spring-loaded plastic bullets. They stung a little when they hit, but that was all. Even up close they barely hurt. I always played the hero, taking the hit for the team. I'd spring out courageously into the line of fire, absorbing one bullet after another. I did a little jump with each successive hit, performing an impromptu interpretive dance. I was really good at it. Inspired by the hero's death, his comrades would launch a bold counterattack. With his noble sacrifice, he'd ensured humanity's salvation. Victory would be declared, and the kids who'd been the bad guys would come back to the human side and everyone would celebrate. There was no game like it.

Pretending to be a hero slain in battle was one thing. Dying a hero in a real war was another. As I got older, I understood the difference, and I knew I didn't wanna die. Not even in a dream.

Some nightmares you can't wake up from, no matter how many times you try. Me, I was trapped in a nightmare, and no matter how many times I woke up, I was still trapped. That I knew I was caught in a loop I couldn't break out of was the worst part of all. I fought back panic.

But was it really happening to me again?

The same day I'd already lived through twice was unfolding again around me. Or maybe it was all a nightmare, after all. Of course things would be happening the way I remembered them. It was all in my head, so why not?

This was ridiculous. I punched the mattress.

Had I dreamed that black point flying at me? Was the javelin that shattered my breastplate and pierced my chest all in my head? Had I imagined the blood, the coughing up bits of lung?

Let me tell you what happens when your lungs are crushed. You drown, not in water, but in air. Gasp as hard as you like, crushed lungs can't pass the oxygen your body needs to your bloodstream. All around you, your friends are breathing in and out without a second thought while you drown alone in a sea of air. I never knew this until it happened to me. I'd never even heard about it. I definitely hadn't made that up. It really happened.

It didn't matter if I never told anyone, if no one ever believed me. It would still be true. The sensation it had imprinted on my mind was proof enough of that. Pain that shoots through your body like a bolt of lightning, legs so damn heavy it feels like they've been stuffed with sandbags, terror so strong it crushes your heart—that's not the stuff of imagination and dreams. I wasn't sure how, but I'd been killed. Twice. No doubt about it.

I didn't mind listening to Yonabaru tell some story I'd already heard before. Hell, I'd do that ten times, a hundred, the more the better. Our daily routines were all filled with that same repetitive shit. But going back into battle? No thanks.

If I stayed here, I'd be killed. Whether I died before or after Yonabaru didn't really matter. There was no way I could survive the firefight. I had to get away. I had to be anywhere but here.

Even saints have limits to their patience, and I was no saint. I'd never been one to blindly believe in God, Buddha, any of that shit, but if somebody up there was going to give me a third chance, I wasn't about to let it go to waste. If I sat here staring up at the top bunk, the only future I had ended in a body bag. If I didn't want to die, I had to move. *Move first, think later.* Just like they taught us in training.

If today was a repetition of yesterday, Ferrell would be around any minute. The first time he showed up I'd been taking a dump, the second I'd been chatting it up with Yonabaru. After that we'd be off to a ridiculous session of PT, and we'd come back exhausted. That got me thinking. Everyone in the 17th Armored would be in that PT. Not only that, everyone else on the base with time on their hands would be gathered around the field to watch. I couldn't have asked for a better chance to sneak out of the base. Considering how tired I'd be after training, it was the only chance I was likely to get.

If I hurt myself, that would probably do it. They wouldn't send a wounded soldier to PT. I needed an injury that looked bad enough to get me out of PT, but nothing so bad it would lay me up. A man with even a shallow scalp wound would gush blood like a stuck pig. It was one of the first things they taught us in First Aid. At the time, I wondered what good first aid or anything else would do after a Mimic javelin had sliced off your head and sent it flying through the air, but I guess you never know when a little piece of knowledge will come in handy. I had to get started quick.

Fuck! I had a whole day to repeat, but I didn't have enough time when I needed it. That blockheaded sergeant was on his way. *Move! Move!*

"What's all that noise down there?" Yonabaru asked casually.

"I gotta head out for a minute."

"Head out? Hey! I need your signature!"

I dove into the space between the bunks without even bothering to tie my shoes. Concrete slapping under my feet, I turned just before hitting the poster of the girl in the swimsuit. I darted past the guy with the porno mag lying on his bed.

I wasn't headed anywhere in particular. Right then my top

priority was making sure I didn't run into Ferrell. I had to get somewhere out of sight where I could hurt myself, then show up covered in blood around the time Yonabaru and Ferrell were finishing their conversation. For a plan I'd cooked up on the fly, it wasn't half bad.

Shit. I should've brought the combat knife I kept under my pillow. It was useless against Mimics, but for opening cans or cutting through wood or cloth, it was something no self-respecting soldier should be without. I'd cut myself with that knife a thousand times during training. I wouldn't have had any trouble making a scalp wound with it.

I'd made it out the entrance of the barracks, and I wanted to put as much space between me and HQ as possible. I let my speed slacken as I rounded the corner of the building.

There was a woman there. Terrible timing.

She grunted as she pushed a cart piled high with potatoes. I knew her: Rachel Kisaragi, a civilian posted over in Cafeteria No. 2. A snow-white bandana, neatly folded into a triangle, covered her black wavy hair. She had healthy, tanned skin and larger than average breasts. Her waist was narrow. Of the three types of women the human race boasted—the pretty, the homely, and the gorillas you couldn't do anything with save ship 'em off to the army—I'd put her in the pretty category without batting an eye.

In a war that had already lasted twenty years, there just wasn't enough money for all the military support staff to be government employees. Even at a base on the front lines, they filled as many noncombatant roles with civilians as they could. The Diet had already debated the possibility of handing over the transport of war matériel in noncombat zones to the private sector. People joked that at this rate, it wouldn't be long before they'd outsource the fighting to civilians and be done with the whole thing.

I'd heard that Rachel was more of a nutritionist than a cook. The only reason I recognized her was that Yonabaru had been chasing her skirt before he hooked up with his current squeeze. Apparently she didn't like guys who were too forward, which pretty much ruled out Yonabaru.

I smirked at the thought and a mountain of potatoes slammed into me. Desperately, I stuck out my right foot to catch my balance, but I slipped on one of the potatoes and went sprawling on my ass. An avalanche of spuds pummeled my face, one after another, the eager jabs of a rookie boxer on his way to the world heavyweight championship. The metal cart delivered the finishing blow, a hard right straight to my temple.

I collapsed to the ground with a thud sufficiently resounding to give a fuel-air grenade a run for its money. It was a while before I could even breathe.

"Are you all right?"

I groaned. At least it looked like none of the potatoes had hit Rachel.

"I . . . I think so."

"Sorry about that. I can't really see where I'm going when I'm pushing this thing."

"Nah, it's not your fault. I jumped out right in front of you."

"Hey, don't I know you?" Rachel peered down at poor flattened me with her green eyes.

A sheepish grin spread across my face. "Looks like we ran into each other again . . ."

"I knew it! You're the new recruit in the 17th."

"Yeah. Sorry for all the trouble," I said. A spud rolled off my belly.

With a hand on her hip, Rachel surveyed the damage. Her delicate eyebrows sank. "Couldn't have spread them out farther if you tried."

"Sorry."

"It's their fault for being so round." She arched her back slightly so her chest stuck out. It was hard to ignore.

"I guess."

"You ever see potatoes that round?"

I hadn't. Not among the tubers littering the floor either.

"Shouldn't take that long to grab them, if you help."

"No—I mean, yeah."

"Well, which is it?"

The clock was ticking. If I wasn't out of here *now*, I'd be dead tomorrow. I didn't have time to stand around grabbing potatoes—or anything else for that matter. But something else was kicking in, an attraction I'd felt for this girl since the first time I'd met her, right after my posting at the base.

I sat there on the ground, stalling and pretending to be in pain.

I was just about to give her my answer when I heard the sound of precisely measured footsteps approaching from behind.

"What are you doing?" came a growl like a hound from the gates of Hell. Ferrell.

He'd appeared from around the corner of the barracks and was now surveying the potatoes strewn across the concrete path with disapproval.

"I-I was pushing my cart, and—"

"This your mess, Kiriya?"

"Sir, yes sir!" I scrambled to my feet. A wave of vertigo washed over me. He rolled his eyes and fixed his gaze on me.

"S-Sir?"

"You're hurt. Let me take a look."

"It's nothing. I'll be fine."

Ferrell stepped closer and touched my head, right at the hairline.

A sharp pain shot across my scalp. His sausage-like fingers pried open the wound. Warm blood spurted from my forehead to the beat of an unseen rock band. The stream ran lazily down the side of my nose, touched the corner of my mouth, then hung briefly on the tip of my chin until a steady *drip drip drip* began. A rose of fresh blood blossomed on the concrete. The sharp smell of iron filled my nostrils. Rachel gasped.

"Hrmm. Nice, clean entry wound. What'd you hit it on?"

Rachel stepped in. "My cart fell over. I'm sorry."

"Is that how it happened?"

"Actually, I'm the one who ran into her, but yeah, pretty much."

"Right. Well, it's not as bad as it looks. You'll be fine," Ferrell said, giving the back of my head a playful slap. A spray of blood flew from my brow, staining my shirt. Leaving me where I was, he walked over to the corner of the barracks and shouted, loud enough to scare the cicadas off the walls, "Yonabaru! Get your butt out here!"

"There some soldierin' needs doin'? I'm here to—oh. Morning, Rachel. Sergeant, another fine day in the corps, I trust? So fine, it looks like the concrete up and sprouted potatoes."

"Shut your piehole and get some men out here to pick these up."

"Who, me?"

"Well he's not going to be picking anything up, is he?" Ferrell nodded in my direction.

Yonabaru gaped. "Dude, what hit you? You look like you went twenty in the cage with a three-hundred-pound Irishman." To the sergeant: "Wait, that means Keiji's the one who knocked all these over?" Back to me: "Helluva way to start the day, goin' and ruinin' a guy's morning like that."

"What's the matter, don't you want to help?"

"Don't be silly! For you, I'd pick up anything. Potatoes, pumpkins, land mines—"

"Enough. Is there anyone in this lousy excuse for a platoon whose head isn't lodged securely up his asshole?"

"That hurts, Sarge. You watch. I'll bring the hardest workin' men in the 17th."

"Kiriya! Quit standin' around like a scarecrow and get your butt over to the infirmary! You're excused from today's PT."

"PT? Who said anything about PT?"

"I did. Someone stepped in a knee-deep pile of pig shit in the PX last night. Now that may not have anything to do with you, but nevertheless, at oh-nine-hundred, you're going to assemble at the No. 1 Training Field in your fourth-tier equipment for Physical Training."

"You gotta be kidding! We're goin' into battle tomorrow, and you're sending us off for PT?"

"That's an order, Corporal."

"Sir, we'll report to the No. 1 Training Field at oh-nine-hundred in full fourth-tier equipment, sir! But one thing, Sarge. We been doin' that liquor raid for years. Why give us a hard time about it now?"

"You really want to know?" Ferrell rolled his eyes.

Leaving the conversation I'd heard before behind, I escaped to the infirmary.

6

I was standing at the gate that divided the base from the outside world. The guard who checked my ID raised his eyebrows doubtfully.

There was an extra layer of security on the base thanks to the U.S. crew's visit. Although the Japanese Corps oversaw general base security, the balance of power with the U.S. prevented them from interfering with anything under U.S. jurisdiction. Luckily, U.S. security didn't have any interest in anyone that wasn't one of their own.

Without leave papers from a commanding officer, Keiji Kiriya wasn't getting off the base. But the U.S .soldiers could come and go as they pleased, and all they had to do was flash an ID. Everyone used the same gate, so if I got an American guard, he might let me through, no questions asked. All they cared about was keeping undesirables away from their precious Special Forces squad. A recruit trying to go AWOL wasn't likely to catch their eye.

The guard must not have seen many Japanese ID cards, because he stared at mine for a long time. The machine that checked IDs just logged who passed through the gate. No need to panic. Why would they change the system up the day before an attack? The muscles in my stomach tensed. The guard was looking back and forth between me and my card, comparing the blurry picture with my face.

The cut on my temple burned. The sawbones who tended to me in the infirmary gave me three stitches without any painkiller. Now it was sending searing bolts of electricity shooting through my body. The bones in my knee creaked.

I was unarmed. I missed my knife, warm and snug under my pillow. If I had it with me, I could lock this guy in a half nelson and—thinking like that wasn't going to get me anywhere. I stretched my back. *Gotta stay cool. If he stares at you, stare right back.*

Stifling a yawn, the guard pressed the button to open the gate. The doorway to freedom creaked open.

I turned slowly to look back as I slipped past the yellow bar. There, in the distance, was the training field. The sea breeze, heavy with the scent of the ocean, blew across the field toward the gate. On the other side of the fence, soldiers the size of ants performed tiny, miniature squats. They were the soldiers I'd eaten with and trained with. They were my friends in the 17th. I swallowed the nostalgia that rose up in me. I walked, unhurried, the moist wind blowing against my body. *Keep walking until you're out of sight of the guard. Don't run. Just a little farther. Turn the corner.* I broke into a sprint.

Once I started running, I didn't stop.

It was fifteen klicks from the base to Tateyama, a nearby entertainment district. Even if I took a roundabout route, it would be twenty klicks at most. Once I was there, I could change my clothes and lay in the supplies I needed. I couldn't risk trains or the highway, but once I hit Chiba City I would be home free. Neither the army nor the police stuck their noses in the underground malls-turned-slums there.

It was about eight hours until Squad 1830's meeting. That's when they'd probably figure out I'd gone AWOL. I didn't know if they'd send cars or choppers after me, but by dusk, I planned to be just another face in the crowd. I remembered the training we'd done at the foot of Mount Fuji. Sixty-kilometer marches in full gear. Crossing the Boso Peninsula in half a day wouldn't be a problem. By the time tomorrow's battle started, I'd be far away from days that repeat themselves and the brutal deaths they ended in.

The sun hung high in the sky, washing me in blinding light. Fifty-seven millimeter automatic guns sat covered in white tarps at hundred-meter intervals along the seawall. Red-brown streaks of rust marred the antique steel plates at their base. The guns had been installed along the entire coastline when the Mimics reached the mainland.

As a kid, when I'd first laid eyes on those guns, I thought they were the coolest things I'd ever seen. The black lacquer finish of their steel instilled an unreasonable sense of confidence in me. Now that I'd seen real battle, I knew with cool certainty that weapons like these could never repel a Mimic attack. These guns moved like the dinosaurs they were. They couldn't hope to land a hit on a Mimic. What a joke.

They still had service crews assigned to these that came out and inspected them once a week. Bureaucracy loves waste.

Maybe humanity would lose.

The thought came to me out of the blue, but I couldn't shake it.

When I told my parents I'd enlisted, they wanted me to join the Coast Guard. They said I'd still get a chance to fight without going into battle. That I'd be performing the vital task of defending the cities where people worked and lived.

But I didn't want to fight the Mimics to save humanity. I'd seen my fill of that in the movies. I could search my soul till my body fell to dust around it and I'd never find the desire to do great things like saving the human race. What I found instead was a wire puzzle you couldn't solve no matter how many times you tried. Something buried under a pile of puzzle pieces that didn't fit. It pissed me off.

I was weak. I couldn't even get the woman I loved—the librarian—to look me in the eye. I thought the irresistible tide of war would change me, forge me into something that worked. I may have fooled myself into believing I'd find the last piece of the puzzle I needed to complete Keiji Kiriya on the battlefield. But I never wanted to be a hero, loved by millions. Not for a minute. If I could convince the few friends I had that I was someone who could do something in this world, who could leave a mark, no matter how small, that would be enough.

And look where that got me.

What had half a year of training done for me? I now possessed a handful of skills that weren't good for shit in a real battle and six-pack abs. I was still weak, and the world was still fucked. *Mom, Dad, I'm sorry. It took me this long to realize the obvious. Ironic that I had to run away from the army before I figured it out.*

The beach was deserted. The Coast Guard must have been busy evacuating this place over the past six months.

After a little less than an hour of running, I planted myself on the edge of the seawall. I'd covered about eight kilometers, putting me about halfway to Tateyama. My sand-colored shirt was dark with sweat. The gauze wrapped around my head was coming loose. A gentle sea breeze—refreshing after that hot wind that had swept across the base—caressed the back of my neck. If it weren't for the machine guns, props stolen from some long forgotten anime, intruding on the real world, it would have been the very picture of a tropical resort.

The beach was littered with the husks of spent firework rockets—the crude kind you put together and launch with a plastic tube. No one would be crazy enough to come this close to a military base to set off fireworks. They must have been left by some bastard on the feed trying to warn the Mimics about the attack on the Boso Peninsula. There were anti-war activists out there who were convinced the Mimics were intelligent creatures, and they were trying to open a line of communication with them. *Ain't democracy grand?*

Thanks to global warming, this whole strip of beach was below sea level when the tide came in. By dusk, these fucking tubes would be washed away by the sea and forgotten. No one would ever know. I kicked one of the melted tubes as hard as I could.

"Well, what's this? A soljer?"

I spun around.

It had been a while since I'd heard anyone speak Japanese. I'd been so lost in my thoughts, I didn't realize anyone had come up behind me.

Two figures, an elderly man and a little girl, stood atop the embankment. The old man's skin would have made fine pickle brine if you set it out in a jar on a bright day like today. In his left hand he clutched a three-pronged metal spear right out of a fairy tale. *What's he doing with a trident?* The girl—she looked about the right age to be in elementary school—squeezed his right hand

tightly. Half hidden behind the man's leg, the girl looked up at me
unabashedly from under her straw hat. The face beneath the hat was
too white to have spent much time cooking under the sun.

"Yourn an unf'milyar face."

"I'm from the Flower Line base." Dammit! I'd run my mouth
before my brain.

"Ah."

"What, uh, brings you two out here?"

"Sea has fish wantin' t'be caught. Family's all gon' up to
Tokyo."

"What happened to the Coast Guard?"

"Word come 'bout the whoopin' we took down on Okinawa.
Why, they all up 'n' left. If the army kin take care them croakers
for us, we'd breathe easier, that's fer sure."

"Yeah." "Croakers" was obviously some local slang for Mimics.
Ordinary people never got the chance to see a Mimic with their
own eyes. At best they'd catch a glimpse of a rotting corpse washed
up on the beach, or maybe one that had gotten caught in a fishing
net and died. But with the conductive sand washed away by the
ocean, all that would remain would be empty husks. That's why a
lot of people thought Mimics were some type of amphibian that
shed its skin.

I only caught about 70 percent of what the old man said, but I
heard enough to know that the Coast Guard had pulled out of the
area. Our defeat at Okinawa must have been more serious than I
thought. Bad enough for them to recall our combined forces up
and down the Uchibo line. Everyone had been redeployed with a
focus on major cities and industrial areas.

The old man smiled and nodded. The girl watched him with
eyes wide as saucers, witness to some rare spectacle. He put a lot
of hope in the UDF troops stationed at Flower Line Base. Not that
I had signed up to defend him or anyone else for that matter. Still,
it made me feel bad.

"You got any smokes, son? Since the mil'tary left, can't hardly come by none."

"Sorry. I don't smoke."

"Then don't you worry none." The old man stared out at the sea.

There weren't many soldiers in the Armored Infantry who suffered from nicotine addiction. Probably because you couldn't smoke during battle, when you needed it the most.

I stood silent. I didn't want to do or say anything stupid. I couldn't let him find out I was a deserter. They shot deserters. Escaping the Mimics just to be killed by the army didn't make much sense.

The girl tugged at the man's hand.

"She tires out real easy. Good eyes on her, though. Been born a boy, she'da been quite a fisherman."

"Yeah."

"Just one thing 'fore I go. Ain't never seen anythin' like this. Came runnin' out my house quick as I might, found you here. What you make of it? Anythin' to do with 'em croakers?" He raised his arm.

My eyes followed the gnarled twigs of his fingers as he pointed. The water had turned green. Not the emerald green you'd see off the shore of some island in the South Pacific, but a frothy, turbid green, as if a supertanker filled with green tea ice cream had run aground and spilled its cargo into the bay. A dead fish floated on the waves, a bright fleck of silver.

I recognized that green. I'd seen it on the monitors during training. Mimics ate soil, just like earthworms. But unlike earthworms, the soil they passed through their bodies and excreted was toxic to other life. The land the Mimics fed on died and turned to desert. The seas turned a milky green.

"Ain't like no red tide I e'er seen."

A high-pitched scream filled the air. My head rang to its familiar tune.

Eyebrows still knitted, the old man's head traced an arc as it sailed through the sky. The shattered pieces of his jaw and neck painted the girl's straw hat a vivid red. She didn't realize what had happened. A javelin exits a Mimic's body at twelve hundred meters per second. The old man's skull went flying before the sound of the javelin had even reached us. She slowly looked up.

A second round sliced through the air. Before her large, dark eyes could take in the sight of her slain grandfather, the javelin ripped through her, an act of neither mercy nor spite.

Her small body was obliterated.

Buffeted by the blast, the old man's headless body swayed. Half his body was stained a deep scarlet. The straw hat spun on the wind. My body recoiled. I couldn't move.

A bloated frog corpse stood at the water's edge.

This coast was definitely within the UDF defense perimeter. I hadn't heard reports of any patrol boats being sunk. The base on the front was alive and well. There couldn't be any Mimics here. A claim the two corpses lying beside me would surely have contested if they could. But they were dead, right before my eyes. And I, their one hope for defense, had just deserted the only military unit in the area capable of holding back this invasion.

I was unarmed. My knife, my gun, my Jacket—they were all back at the base. When I'd walked through that gate an hour ago, I'd left my only hope for defense behind. Thirty meters to the nearest 57mm gun. Within running distance. I knew how to fire one, but there was still the tarp to deal with. I'd never have time to get it off. Insert my ID card into the platform, key in my passcode, feed in a thirty kilometer ammo belt, release the rotation lock lever or the barrel won't move and I can't aim, climb into the seat, crank the rusted handle—fuck it. *Fire, motherfucker! Fire!*

I knew the power of a Mimic. They weighed several times as much as a fully geared Jacket jockey. Structurally they had a lot in common with a starfish. There was an endoskeleton just below the skin, and it took 50mm armor-piercing rounds or better to penetrate it. And they didn't hold back just because a man was unarmed. They rolled right through you like a rototiller through a gopher mound.

"Fuck me."

The first javelin pierced my thigh.

The second opened a gaping wound in my back.

I was too busy trying to keep down the organs that came gurgling up into my throat to even notice the third.

I blacked out.

ㄱ

The paperback I'd been reading was beside my pillow. Yonabaru was counting his bundle of confessions on the top bunk.

"Keiji, sign this."

"Corporal, you have a sidearm, don't you?"

"Yeah."

"Could I see it?"

"Since when are you a gun nut?"

"It's not like that."

His hand disappeared into the top bunk. When it returned, it clutched a glistening lump of black metal.

"It's loaded, so watch where you point it."

"Uh, right."

"If you make corporal, you can bring your own toys to bed and ain't nobody can say a thing about it. Peashooter like this ain't no good against a Mimic anyhow. The only things a Jacket jockey needs are his 20mm and his rocket launcher, three rockets apiece. The banana he packs for a snack doesn't count. Now would you sign this already?"

I was too busy flicking off the safety on the gun to answer.

I wrapped my mouth around the barrel, imagining that 9mm slug in the chamber, waiting to explode from the cold, hard steel.

I pulled the trigger.

8

The paperback I'd been reading was beside my pillow. I sighed.

"Keiji, sign this." Yonabaru craned his neck down from the top bunk.

"Sir, yes sir."

"Listen. There's nothin' to tomorrow's operation. Sweat it too much, you'll turn into a feedhead—end up losing your mind before they even get a chance to blow your brains out."

"I'm not sweating anything."

"Hey man, ain't nothin' to be ashamed of. Everyone's nervous their first time. It's like gettin' laid. Until you've done the deed, you can't get it out of your head. All you can do is pass the time jerkin' off."

"I disagree."

"Hey, you're talkin' to a man who's played the game."

"What if—just hypothetically—you kept repeating your first time over and over?"

"Where'd you get that shit?"

"I'm just talkin' hypothetically is all. Like resetting all the pieces on a chess board. You take your turn, then everything goes back to how it started."

"It depends." Still hanging from the top bunk, his face lit up. "You talkin' about fucking or fighting?"

"No fucking."

"Well, if they asked me to go back and fight at Okinawa again, I'd tell 'em to shove it up their asses. They could send me to a fuckin' firing squad if they want, but I wouldn't go back."

What if you didn't have a choice? What if you had to relive your execution again and again?

At the end of the day, every man has to wipe his own ass. There's no one to make your decisions for you, either. And whatever situation you're in, that's just another factor in your decision. Which isn't to say everybody gets the same range of choices as everybody else. If there's one guy out there with an ace in the hole, there's sure to be another who's been dealt a handful of shit. Sometimes you run into a dead end. But you walked each step of the road that led you there on your own. Even when they string you up on the gallows, you have the choice to meet your death with dignity or go kicking and screaming into the hereafter.

But I didn't get that choice. There could be a giant waterfall just beyond Tateyama, the edge of the whole damn world, and I'd never know it. Day after day I go back and forth between the base and the battlefield, where I'm squashed like a bug crawling on the ground. So long as the wind blows, I'm born again, and I die. I can't take anything with me to my next life. The only things I get to keep are my solitude, a fear that no one can understand, and the feel of the trigger against my finger.

It's a fucked-up world, with fucked-up rules. So fuck it.

I took a pen from beside my pillow and wrote the number "5" on the back of my left hand. My battle begins with this number.

Let's see how much I can take with me. So what if the world hands me a pile of shit? I'll comb through it for the corn. I'll dodge enemy bullets by a hair's breadth. I'll slaughter Mimics with a single blow. If Rita Vrataski is a goddess on the battlefield, I'll watch and learn until I can match her kill for kill. I have all the time in the world.

Nothing better to do.

Who knows? Maybe something will change. Or maybe, I'll find a way to take this fucking world and piss in its eye.

That'd be just fine by me.

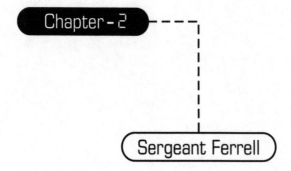

Chapter - 2

Sergeant Ferrell

2

¦

"If a cat can catch mice," a Chinese emperor once said, "it's a good cat."

Rita Vrataski was a very good cat. She killed her share and was duly rewarded. I, on the other hand, was a mangy alley cat padding listlessly through the battlefield, all ready to be skinned, gutted, and made into a tennis racquet. The brass made sure Rita stayed neatly groomed, but they didn't give a rat's ass about the rest of us grunts.

PT had been going on for three grueling hours, and you can be damn sure it included some fucking iso push-ups. I was so busy trying to figure out what to do next that I wasn't paying attention to the here and now. After half an hour, U.S. Special Forces gave up on watching our tortures and went back to the barracks. I kept from staring at Rita, and she left along with the rest, which meant I was in for the long haul. It was like a software if/then routine:

> *If checkflag* RitajoinsPT *=true, then end.*
> *Else continue routine:* FuckingIsoPush-Ups

Maybe this was proof that I *could* change what happened. If I stared at Rita, she'd join the PT, and they'd end it after an hour. The brass had convened this session of PT for no good reason; they could end it for the same.

If my guess were right, my cause wasn't necessarily hopeless. A window of opportunity might present itself in tomorrow's battle. The odds of that happening might be 0.1 percent, or even 0.01 percent, but if I could improve my combat skills even the slightest bit—if that window were to open even a crack—I'd find a way to force it open wide. If I could train to jump every hurdle this little track meet of death threw at me, maybe someday I'd wake up in a world with a tomorrow.

Next time I'd be sure to stare at Rita during PT. I felt a little bad about bringing her into this, she who was basically a bystander in my endless one-man show. But there wasn't really much choice. I didn't have hours to waste building muscle that didn't carry over into the next loop. That was time better spent programming my brain for battle.

When the training had finally finished, the men on the field fled to the barracks to escape the sun's heat, grumbling complaints under their collective breath. I walked over to Sergeant Ferrell who was crouched down retying his shoelaces. He'd been around longer than any of us, so I decided he'd be the best place to start for help on my battle-training program. Not only was he the longest surviving member of the platoon, but it occurred to me that the 20 percent drill sergeant he had in him might just come in handy.

Waves of heat shimmered above his flattop haircut. Even after three hours of PT, he looked as though he could run a triathlon and come in first without breaking a sweat. He had a peculiar scar at the base of his thick neck, a token from the time before they'd worked all the bugs out of the Jackets and had had to implant chips to heighten soldiers' reaction times. It had been a while since they'd had to resort to anything so crude. That scar was a medal of honor—twenty years of hard service and still kicking.

"Any blisters today?" Ferrell's attention never left his shoes. He spoke Burst with a roll of the tongue peculiar to Brazilians.

"No."

"Getting cold feet?"

"I'd be lying if I said I wasn't scared, but I'm not planning on running, if that's what you mean."

"For a greenhorn fresh out of basic, you're shaping up just fine."

"You still keep up with your training, don't you, Sarge?"

"Try to."

"Would you mind if I trained with you?"

"You attempting some kind of humor, Private?"

"Nothing funny about killing, sir."

"Well, there's something funny with your head if you want to stuff yourself into one of those damn Jackets the day before we head out to die. You want to work up a sweat, go find a coed's thighs to do it in." Ferrell's eyes stayed on his laces. "Dismissed."

"Sarge? With all due respect, I don't see you running after the ladies."

Ferrell finally looked up. His eyes were 20mm rifle barrels firing volleys at me from the bunkers set deep in the lines of his tanned, leathery face. I cooked under the glaring sun.

"You tellin' me you think I'm some sort of faggot who'd rather be strapped into a Jacket reeking of sweat than up between a woman's legs? That what you're tellin' me?"

"Tha-that's—not what I meant, sir!"

"Right, then. Take a seat." He ran his hand through his hair and patted the ground.

I sat down as a gust of ocean wind blew between us.

"I was on Ishigaki, you know," Ferrell began. "Musta been at least ten years ago. Jackets back then were cheap as hell. There was this place near the crotch—right about here—where the plates didn't meet quite right. Rubbed right through your skin. And the places that had scabbed over during training would rub through again when you got into battle. Hurt so bad some guys refused to crawl on the ground. They'd get up and walk right in the middle of a fight. You could tell 'em it would get 'em killed, but there were always a few who got up anyway. Might as well have walked around with targets painted on their chests." Ferrell whistled like a falling shell. "Whap! Lost a bunch of men that way."

Ferrell had a mix of Japanese and Brazilian blood in him, but he came from South America. Half that continent had been ravaged by the Mimics. Here in Japan, where high-tech was cheaper than good food, our Jackets were precision pieces of machinery. Still, there were plenty of countries where it was all they could do to send their troops off with a gas mask, a good old-fashioned rocket launcher, and a prayer. Forget about artillery or air support. Any victory they did happen to win was short-lived. Nanobots spilling from Mimic corpses would eat the lungs out of whatever soldiers were left. And so, little by little, lifeless desert spread through the lands people once called home.

Ferrell came from a family of farmers. When their crops started to fail, they chose to abandon their land and move to one of the islands in the east, safe havens protected by the wonders of technology. Families with people serving in the UDF were given priority for immigration, which is how Ferrell came to join the Japanese Corps.

These "Immigration Soldiers," as they were known, were common in the Armored Infantry.

"You ever hear the expression *kiri-oboeru?*"

"What?" I asked, startled to hear the Japanese.

"It's an old samurai saying that means 'Strike down your enemy, and learn.'"

I shook my head. "Doesn't sound familiar."

"Tsukahara Bokuden, Itou Itousai, Miyamato Musashi—all famous samurai in their day. We're talking five hundred years ago, now."

"I think I read a comic about Musashi once."

"Damn kids. Wouldn't know Bokuden from Batman." Ferrell sighed in exasperation. There I was, pure-blooded Japanese, and he knew more about my country's history than I did. "Samurai were warriors who earned their living fighting, just like you and me. How many people do you think the samurai I just named killed in their lifetimes?"

"I dunno. If their names are still around after five hundred years, maybe . . . ten or twenty?"

"Not even close. The records from back then are sketchy, but the number is somewhere between three and five hundred. Each. They didn't have guns. They didn't have bombs. Every single man they killed they cut down in hand-to-fucking-hand combat. I'd say that'd be enough to warrant a medal or two."

"How'd they do it?"

"Send one man to the great beyond each week, then do the same for ten years, you'll have your five hundred. That's why they're known as master swordsmen. They didn't just kill once and call it a day. They kept going. And they got *better*."

"Sounds like a video game. The more you kill, the stronger you get—that it? Shit, I got a lot of catching up to do."

"Except their opponents weren't training dummies or little digital aliens. These were living, breathing men they slaughtered. Like cattle. Men with swords. Men fighting for their lives, same as them. If they wanted to live, they had to catch their enemy off-guard, lay traps, and sometimes run away with their tail between their legs."

Not the first image that sprang into your head when you thought of master swordsmen.

"Learning what would get you killed and how to get your enemy killed—the only way to know a thing like that is to do it. Some kid who'd been taught how to swing a sword in a dojo didn't stand a chance against a man who'd been tested in battle. They knew it, and they kept doing it. That's how they piled up hundreds of corpses. One swing at a time."

"*Kiri-oboeru.*"

"That's right."

"So why do they bother training us at all?"

"Ah, right to the point. Brains like that, you're too smart to be a soldier."

"Whatever, Sarge."

"If you really want to fight the Mimics, you need helicopters or tanks. But helicopters cost money, and it takes money to train the pilots, too. And tanks won't do you a lick of good on this terrain— too many mountains and rivers. But Japan is crawling with people. So they wrap 'em in Jackets and ship 'em to the front lines. Lemons into lemonade."

Look what happened to the lemons.

"All that shit they drum into you in training is the bare minimum. They take a bunch of recruits who don't know their assholes from their elbows and teach 'em not to cross the street when the light's red. Look left, look right, and keep your heads down when things get hot. Most unlucky bastards forget all that when the shit starts flying and they go down pretty quick. But if you're lucky, you might live through it and maybe even learn something. Take your first taste of battle and make a lesson out of it, you might just have something you can call a soldier—" Ferrell cut himself off. "What's so funny?"

"Huh?" A smirk had crept across my face while he was talking and I didn't even notice.

"I see someone grinning like that before a battle, I start worrying about the wiring in his head."

I'd been thinking of my first battle, when Mad Wargarita tried to help me, when my mud-stained guts were burnt to cinders, when despair and fear streamed down my face. Keiji Kiriya had been one of the unlucky bastards. Twice.

The third time, when I ran, my luck hadn't been what you'd call good either. But for some reason, the world kept giving me another chance, challenging me to find a way to survive. Not by luck, but on my own.

If I could suppress the urge to run, I'd keep waking up to a full day of training followed by a day on the battlefield. And what could be better than that? Almost by default, I'd keep learning, one swing at a time. What took those swordsmen ten years, I could do in a day.

Ferrell stood and gave my backside a slap with his hand, bringing my train of thought to a screeching halt. "Not much point worrying about it now. Why don't you see about finding one of them coeds?"

"I'm fine, Sarge, I was just thinking—" Ferrell looked away. I pressed on. "If I live through tomorrow's battle, there'll be another battle after that, right? And if I live through that battle, I'll go on to the next one. If I take the skills I learn in each battle, and in between battles I practice in the simulators, my odds of surviving should keep going up. Right?"

"Well, if you want to overanalyze—"

"It can't hurt to get in the habit of training now, can it?"

"You don't give up easy, do you?"

"Nope."

Ferrell shook his head. "To be honest, I had you figured for someone different. Maybe I'm gettin' too old for this."

"Different how?"

"Listen, there are three kinds of people in the UDF: junkies so strung out they're hardly alive, people who signed up looking for a meal ticket, and people who were walking along, took a wrong step off a bridge somewhere, and just landed in it."

"I'm guessing you had me pegged for the last group."

"That I did."

"Which group were you in, Sarge?"

He shrugged. "Suit up in first-tier gear. Meet back here in fifteen minutes."

"Sir—uh, full battle dress?"

"A Jacket jockey can't practice without his equipment. Don't worry, I won't use live rounds. Now suit up!"

"Sir, yes sir!"

I saluted, and I meant it.

The human body is a funny machine. When you want to move something—say, your arm—the brain actually sends two signals at the same time: "More power!" and "Less power!" The operating system that runs the body automatically holds some power back to avoid overexerting and tearing itself apart. Not all machines have that built-in safety feature. You can point a car at a wall, slam the accelerator to the floor, and the car will crush itself against the wall until the engine is destroyed or runs out of gas.

Martial arts use every scrap of strength the body has at its disposal. In martial arts training, you punch and shout at the same time. Your "Shout louder!" command helps to override the "Less power!" command. With practice, you can throttle the amount of power your body holds back. In essence, you're learning to channel the body's power to destroy itself.

A soldier and his Jacket work the same way. Just like the human body has a mechanism to hold power back, Jackets have a system to keep the power exertion in balance. With 370 kilograms of force in the grip, a Jacket could easily crush a rifle barrel, not to mention human bone. To prevent accidents like that from happening, Jackets are designed to automatically limit the force exerted, and even actively counteract inertia to properly balance the amount of force delivered. The techs call this system the auto-balancer. The auto-balancer slows the Jacket operator's actions by a fraction of a second. It's an interval of time so minute that most people wouldn't even notice it. But on the battlefield, that interval could spell the difference between life and death.

In three full battles of ten thousand Jackets each, only one soldier might have the misfortune of encountering a problem with the auto-balancer, and if the auto-balancer decides to hiccup right when you've got a Mimic bearing down on you, it's all over. It's a slight chance, but no one wants to be the unlucky bastard who draws the short straw. This is why, at the start of every battle, veterans like Ferrell switch the auto-balancer off. They never taught us this in training. I had to learn how to walk again with the auto-balancer turned off. Ferrell said I had to be able to move without thinking.

It took me seven tries to walk in a straight line.

2

Two sentries were posted on the road leading to the section of the base under U.S. jurisdiction. They were huge, each man carrying a high-power rifle in arms as big around as my thighs.

Their physiques made them look like suits of armor on display. They didn't have to say a word to let passersby know who was in charge. Cluster bombs could have rained from the sky, and these guys would have held their ground, unblinking, until they received direct orders to do otherwise.

If you kept them in the corner of your eye and headed for the main gate, you'd be on the path I'd taken when I tried going AWOL on my third time through the loop. Running would be easy. With what I'd learned, I could probably avoid the Mimic ambush and make it to Chiba City. But today I had another objective in mind.

It was 10:29. I was standing in the sentries' blind spot. With my eighty-centimeter stride, the sentries were exactly fifteen seconds from where I stood.

A gull flew overhead. The distant roar of the sea blended with the sounds of the base. My shadow was a small pool collected at my feet. There was no one else on the path.

An American fuel truck passed by. The sentries saluted.

I had to time my walk just right.

Three, two, one.

The truck approached a fork in the road. An old cleaning lady carrying a mop stepped out in front of the truck. Brakes squealed. The truck's engine stalled. The sentries turned toward the commotion, their attentions diverted for a few precious moments.

I walked right by.

I could feel the heat cast by their sheer bulk. With muscles like that, I had no doubt they could reach up my ass and yank out my spine. For an instant, I felt an irrational desire to lash out against them.

Sure, I might look like I'd blow over in a stiff wind, but you shouldn't judge a book by its cover. Want to try me? Who wants a piece of the little Asian recruit?

Would the skills I'd learned to pilot a Jacket translate to hand-to-hand

*combat against another human? Had I gotten any stronger, any better? Why
wait for the Mimics, why not test myself on these fine specimens now?*

The guard on the right turned.

*Stay calm. Keep your pace steady. He's pivoting to the left. When he does,
you'll slip into his blind spot behind the other sentry. By the time he looks
around for any sign of Keiji Kiriya, I'll be part of the scenery.*

"Did you see something?"

"Quiet. Captain's watchin', and he don't look happy."

"Fuck you."

And like that, I'd infiltrated U.S. territory.

My target was a U.S.-made Jacket. After a few times through
the loop, I'd come to the conclusion that I needed a new weapon—
something we didn't have in the Japanese Corps. The standard-issue
20mm rifles weren't very effective against Mimics. They walked a
thin line of compromise between the number of rounds a soldier
could carry, the rate of fire necessary to hit a fast-moving target,
and the acceptable amount of recoil. They were more powerful than
the weapons they used to issue, but if you really wanted to pierce
that endoskeleton, 50mm was the only way to be sure.

The basic UDF strategy was to employ a line of prone armored
infantry firing 20mm rounds to slow the enemy enough so that
artillery and tanks could take them out. In practice, the support
never came fast or heavy enough. It fell to us to finish the Mimics
on our own.

The weapon of last resort for the old-timers, and one I'd used
myself, was the pile driver mounted on the left shoulder. You could
punch open a hole and spill a Mimic's guts with one of those babies.
The rocket launcher could come in handy too, but it was hard to
a score a hit with, and more often than not you'd be out of rockets
when you really needed one. As I grew accustomed to the fighting,
I relied more and more on the power of the 57mm pile driver.

But the pile driver had one major drawback: Its magazine only held
twenty charges. Unlike our rifles, you couldn't change magazines,

either. Once you fired that twentieth round, you were finished. At best, a soldier was going to punch twenty holes in something. Once the pile driver was out of charges, you couldn't even use it to drive a stake into the heart of a vampire. The people who'd designed the Jacket just hadn't considered the possibility that someone would survive long enough in hand-to-hand combat with a Mimic to use more than twenty rounds.

Fuck that.

Running out of charges had killed me plenty of times. Another dead end. The only way to avoid it was to find a melee weapon that didn't run out of ammo. I'd seen one, once, in the battle that had started this whole loop.

The battle axe. Rita Vrataski, a Valkyrie clad in a crimson Jacket, and her axe. It might have been more appropriate to call it a slab of tungsten carbide in the shape of an axe. A battle axe never ran out of ammo. You could still use it if it got bent. It packed plenty of punch. It was the perfect melee weapon.

But as far as the world was concerned, Keiji Kiriya was a new recruit who had yet to see his first battle. If I asked them to replace my standard-issue pile driver with a different weapon simply because I didn't like it, they sure as hell weren't going to listen. Yonabaru had laughed at me, and Ferrell actually threw a punch. When I tried taking it straight to our platoon commander, he ignored me completely. I was going to have to acquire the weapon I needed on my own.

I headed for the barracks of the supply division that had accompanied U.S. Special Forces. Five minutes after crossing into the U.S. side of the base, I came to a spot guarded by only one soldier. She was twirling a monkey wrench in her hand.

The pungent scent of oil drifted in the air, swamping the ocean's briny tang. The ever present drone of men bustling about the base had receded. In the darkness of the barracks, the steel weapons humanity used to strike down its enemies were enjoying a short nap.

The woman with the wrench was Shasta Raylle, a civilian tech. Her pay was at least on par with a first lieutenant. Way above mine, at any rate. I'd snuck a look at her papers: height, 152 centimeters; weight, 37 kilograms; visual acuity, 20/300; favorite food, passion-fruit cake. She had some American Indian blood in her and wore her black hair pulled back in a ponytail.

If Rita was a lynx on the prowl, Shasta was an unsuspecting rabbit. She belonged at home, curled up in a warm, cozy room watching vids and stuffing her face with bonbons, not smeared with oil and grease on some military base.

I spoke as gently as I could. "Hello."

Shasta jumped at the sound of my voice. Damn. Not gentle enough.

Her thick glasses fell to the concrete floor. Watching her look for those glasses was like watching a quadriplegic tread water. Instead of putting down the monkey wrench and feeling for them with both hands, she groped in vain with just the one. Not exactly what you'd expect from someone who'd graduated top of her class at MIT, developed some of the most advanced military Jackets at her first defense industry research post, and then, for an encore, leapt into the UDF as the crack technician assigned to a particular gunmetal red Jacket.

I bent over and picked up her glasses—more like a pair of magnifying lenses that had been jury-rigged together.

"You dropped these," I said, holding them up where I hoped she could see.

"Thank you, whoever you are."

"Don't mention it."

Shasta looked me over. The glass-bottle lenses made fried eggs of her eyes.

"And you are . . .?"

"Keiji Kiriya."

"Thank you, Keiji Kiriya. I'm Shasta Raylle." I had deliberately left out my rank and platoon. Shasta's head sank. "I realize this might look like a plain, ordinary barracks—well, it is, but that's beside the point. The point *is*, it contains highly sensitive military technology. Only people with the appropriate security clearance are allowed in."

"I know. I don't want in."

"Oh. Well! I'm glad we cleared that up."

"Actually," I said, taking a step forward, "I came to see you."

"Me? I-I'm flattered, but I'm afraid I can't—I mean, you seem very nice and all, it's just that I don't think this would be appropriate, and there are still preparations to be made for tomorrow, and—"

"It's not even noon."

"It will take the rest of the day!"

"If you'd just listen—"

"I know it *looks* as though all I've been doing is removing and reattaching this one part—and well I have, but I really *am* busy. Really!" Her ponytail bobbed as she nodded to herself, punctuating her sincerity.

She's getting the wrong idea. Got to steer this thing back on course—

"So the external memory unit on that suit's been damaged?"

"It has, but—how did you know that?"

"Hey, you and I both know that an external memory unit doesn't see a whole lotta use in battle. But since those custom chips contain sensitive military technology by the metric ton, you have to fill out a mountain of paperwork to requisition one of the damn things, am I right? And that bald sonofabitch over at the armory hitting on you no matter how many times you tell him you're not interested doesn't make the situation any brighter, I'm guessing. It's almost enough to make you consider stealing one off one of the Japanese Corps' Jackets."

"Stealing one of the—I'd never even think of it!"

"No?"

"Of course not! Well, the thought may have crossed my mind

once or twice, but I'd never actually *do* it! Do I really look like the type to—" Her eyes widened as she saw what was in the sealed plastic bag I pulled from my pocket.

A sly grin spread across my face. "What if someone else stole one for you?"

"Could I have it? Please?"

"How soon we change our song!"

I raised the bag containing the chip high above my head. Shasta hopped as she tried to grab it, but she and her 158 centimeters were out of luck. The oil staining her clothes made my nostrils flare.

"Stop teasing me and just hand it over, would you?"

Hop. Hop.

"You don't know how much I had to go through to get this."

"I'm begging you. Please?"

Hop.

"I'll give it to you, but I need something in exchange."

"Something . . . in exchange?"

Gulp.

She clutched the monkey wrench to her chest, flattening the swells of her breasts that lay hidden beneath her overalls. She'd clearly gotten used to playing the victim after a few years with the animals in Special Forces. If it was this easy to get a rise out of her, I can't say I blamed them.

I waved the plastic bag toward the giant battle axe hanging from a cage at the rear of the barracks and pointed. Shasta didn't seem to understand what I was looking at. Her eyes darted warily around the room.

"I came to borrow that." I jabbed my finger straight at the axe.

"Unless my eyes have gotten worse than I thought, that's Rita's battle axe."

"Bingo."

"So . . . you're in the Armored Infantry too?"

"Japanese Corps."

"This isn't easy for me to say—I don't want to be rude—but trying to imitate Rita will only get you hurt."

"That mean you won't loan it to me?"

"If you really think you'll need it, I will. It's just a hunk of metal—we have plenty of spares. When Rita first asked me for one, I had them cut from the wings of a decommissioned bomber."

"So why the reluctance?"

"Well, because frankly, you'll be killed."

"With or without it, I'll die someday."

"I can't change your mind?"

"Not likely."

Shasta grew quiet. The wrench hung in her hand like an old rag, and her eyes lost focus. A lock of unkempt hair stuck to the sweat and grease smeared across her forehead. "I was stationed in North Africa before," she said. "The best soldier of the best platoon down there asked me for the same thing as you. I tried to warn him, but there were politics involved, things got complicated, so I let him have it."

"And he died?"

"No, he lived. Barely. But his soldiering days were over. If only I could have found some way to stop him."

"You shouldn't blame yourself. You didn't make the Mimics attack."

"That's just it, he wasn't injured fighting the Mimics. Do you know what inertia is?"

"I've got a high school diploma."

"Each of those battle axes weighs 200 kilograms. A Jacket's 370 kilogram grip can hold on to it, sure, but even with enhanced strength that's a tremendous amount of inertia. He broke his back swinging the axe. If you swing 200 kilograms with the amplified power of a Jacket, you can literally twist yourself into two pieces."

I knew exactly what she meant—the inertia she was talking about was exactly what I was after. It took something massive to shatter a Mimic endoskeleton in one hit. That it could kill me in the process was beside the point.

"Look, I'm sure you think you're good, but Rita's no ordinary soldier." Shasta made one final attempt to dissuade me.

"I know."

"She's *extra*ordinary, really. She never uses her auto-balancer. And I don't mean she turns it off before battle. Her Jacket isn't even equipped with one. She's the only member of our squad without it. In an elite squad, she's more than elite."

"I quit using an auto-balancer a long time ago. I never thought about removing it entirely. I'll have to do that. Less weight."

"Oh, so you're the next Rita, I suppose?"

"No. I couldn't hold a candle to Rita Vrataski."

"You know what she told me the first time I met her? She said she was glad she lived in a world full of war. Can you say the same?" Shasta appraised me from behind her thick lenses. I knew she meant what she was saying. I returned her stare without a word.

"Why are you so hung up about her battle axe?" she asked.

"I wouldn't say I'm hung up about it. I'm just trying to find something more effective than a pile driver. I'll take a spear or a cutlass, if you have one. Anything I can use more than twenty times."

"That's what she said when she first asked me to cut her the axe." Shasta relaxed her grip on the monkey wrench.

"Any comparison with the Full Metal Bi—uh, Valkyrie is high praise."

"You know, you're very . . ." Her voice trailed off.

"I'm very what?"

"Unusual."

"Maybe so."

"Just remember, it's not an easy weapon to use."

"I have a lot of time to practice."

Shasta smiled. "I've met soldiers who think they can follow in Rita's footsteps and fail, and I've met some who recognize her for the prodigy she is and never even try to match her. But you're the first person I've met who realizes the distance between themselves and Rita and yet is prepared to run it."

The more I understood war, the more I knew just what a prodigy Rita was. The second time through the loop, when Rita joined us in the PT session, I'd only stared at her the way I had because I was a new recruit who didn't know any better. Now that I'd been through the loop enough times to call myself a real Jacket jockey, the gap between her and me seemed even greater. If I didn't have, literally, an infinite amount of time, I would have given up.

With a magnificent leap, Shasta plucked the silicon chip from my hand. "Hang on. Let me give you some papers for that axe before you go."

"Thanks."

She made to leave for the papers, then stopped. "Can I ask you something?"

"Shoot."

"Why do you have the number forty-seven written on your hand?"

I didn't know what to tell her. On the spot, I couldn't come up with a single believable reason a soldier would have to write a number on his hand.

"Oh, was that—I mean, I hope I didn't say anything I shouldn't have?"

I shook my head. "You know how people cross off days on a calendar? It's something like that."

"If it's important enough to write it on your hand, it must be something you don't want to forget. Forty-seven days till you go home, maybe? Or the days until your girlfriend's birthday?"

"If I had to put a name to it, I'd say it's the number of days since I died."

Shasta didn't say anything else.

I had my battle axe.

3

0600	Wake up.
0603	Ignore Yonabaru.
0610	Steal silicon chip from armory.
0630	Eat breakfast.
0730	Practice basic body movement.
0900	Visualize training during fucking PT.
1030	Borrow battle axe from Shasta.
1130	Eat lunch.
1300	Train with emphasis on correcting mistakes of previous battle. (In Jacket.)
1500	Meet Ferrell for live battle training. (In Jacket.)
1745	Eat dinner.
1830	Attend platoon meeting.
1900	Go to Yonabaru's party.
2000	Check Jacket.
2200	Go to bed.
0112	Help Yonabaru into his bunk.

This was more or less how I spent my day.

Outside of training, everything had become routine. I'd snuck past those sentries so many times I could do it with my eyes closed. I was starting to worry that I'd become a master thief before I made it as a professional soldier. Not that the ability to steal anything in a world that resets itself at the end of every other day would do much good.

The daily grind didn't change much from one pass through the loop to the next. If I strayed really far from the routine, I could force something different to happen, but if I didn't do anything it would play out the same as always. It was like everyone kept reading from the same script they'd been given the day before and ad-libbing was frowned upon.

It was 1136 and I was eating lunch in Cafeteria No. 2. The lunch lady served me the same amount of onion soup at the same time in the same bowl. I moved my arm to avoid the same splash as it traced the same arc through the air. Dodging calls from friends throughout the cafeteria, I sat in the same seat.

Rita was sitting three rows in front of me, her back to me as she ate. I hadn't chosen this time to eat because it coincided with her lunch; it just worked out that way. For no particular reason, I'd gotten used to watching her eat from this same angle each day.

Cafeteria No. 2 wasn't the sort of place a sergeant major like Rita would normally be expected to dine. It's not that the food was bad. It was pretty good, actually. But it didn't seem likely to impress someone who woke up in an officer's private sky lounge each morning and had half the base at her beck and call. I'd even heard that U.S. Special Forces had brought along their own cook, which only deepened the mystery of her presence. She could have swallowed a live rat and wouldn't have seemed more a snake in our midst. And so our savior ate alone. No one tried to talk to her, and the seats around her were always conspicuously empty.

For all her prowess in battle, Rita Vrataski ate like a child. She licked the soup from the corners of her mouth and drew pictures in her food with the tips of her chopsticks. Apparently chopsticks were something new to her. At 1143 she dropped a bean on her plate. It rolled, picking up speed, bouncing first to her tray, and then to the table. The bean flew through the air with a clockwise spin, careening toward the concrete floor. Every time, with lightning reflexes, Rita would extend her left hand, pluck the bean out of the air, and cram it into her mouth. All in under 0.11 seconds. If she'd lived back in the Old West, I imagine she'd have outdrawn Billy the Kid. If she'd been a samurai, she could have read every flash of Kojiro Sasaki's katana. Even when she was eating, the Full Metal Bitch was the Full Metal Bitch.

Today, like every day, she was trying to eat an *umeboshi* pickled plum. She must have confused it for an ordinary piece of dried fruit. After two or three attempts to pick it up with her chopsticks, she put the whole thing in her mouth.

Down the hatch.

Rita doubled over as though she'd taken a 57mm round right in the gut. Her back twitched. Her rust-colored hair looked like it was about to stand on end. But she didn't cough it back up. Tough as nails. She had swallowed the whole thing, pit and all. Rita gulped down a glass of water with a vengeance.

She must have been at least twenty-two years old, but you'd never guess it watching her. The sand-colored military uniforms didn't flatter her, but if you dressed her up in one of those frilly numbers the girls in town were wearing, she'd be pretty cute. At least I liked to imagine so.

What's wrong with this food? It tastes like paper.

"You enjoyin' yourself?" The voice came from above my head.

Holding my chopsticks without moving a muscle, I looked out the corner of my eye. A prehistoric face looked down at me from beneath a flattop haircut that leveled off about two meters above sea level. His features were more dinosaur than human. Definitely some velociraptor lurking in that family tree. My spirits fell when I saw the tattoo on his shoulder: a wolf wearing a crown. He was from the 4th, the company holding a grudge against us over that rugby game. I went back to lifting food to my mouth with machine-like regularity.

He raised his eyebrows, two plump bushes that would have been the envy of the caterpillar world. "I asked if you were enjoyin' yourself."

"How could I not enjoy myself in such fine company?"

"So how come you're gulpin' down your chow like it was something you found stuck on the end of a toilet brush?"

There were only a handful of soldiers sitting at the oversized tables in the cafeteria. The smell of something sweet wafted from the kitchen. Artificial light from the fluorescents in the ceiling washed over the fried shrimp heaped onto our heavy-duty plates.

If you had to categorize the food prepared in the UDF as good or bad, it was definitely good. There were only three things a soldier in the UDF did, after all: eat, sleep, and fight. If the food wasn't good you'd have a morale problem on your hands. And according to Yonabaru, the food on Flower Line Base was better than most.

The first time I tasted it, I thought it was delicious. That was about five subjective months ago now, maybe more. About a month into the loop, I started heavily seasoning my food. The intentionally mismatched condiments created a taste just horrible enough to remind me the food was there. And now, even that had stopped working. I don't care if you're eating food prepared by a four-star chef, after eighty days of the same thing, it all tastes alike. Probably because it is. By that point, it was hard for me to think of food as anything other than a source of energy.

"If the look on my face put you off your lunch, I apologize." No use trying to start a fight.

"Hold it. You tryin' to say this is *my* fault?"

"I don't have time for this."

I started shoveling the rest of the food on my plate into my mouth. He slammed a palm the size of a baseball glove down on the table. Onion soup splashed on my shirt, leaving a stain where the lunch lady's best efforts had failed. I didn't really mind. No matter how tough the stain was, it would be gone by tomorrow, and I wouldn't even have to wash it.

"Fourth Company grunts not worth the time of the mighty 17th, that it?"

I realized I'd unwittingly set a very annoying flag. This loop had been cursed from the get-go, really. I had accidentally killed Ferrell at the end of the last loop, and that had thrown everything out of whack this time around. From where I was, it hadn't even been five hours since he'd died vomiting blood. Of course I'd been KIA too, but that was to be expected. Ferrell had died trying to protect a fucking new recruit. It had been just the spur my migraine needed to kick into a gallop.

I'd planned to ease my mind by staring at Rita the way I always did, but my foul mood must have been more obvious than I realized. Clearly, it was bad enough to trigger something that hadn't happened in any of the previous loops.

I picked up my tray and stood.

The man's body was a wall of meat blocking my way. People started to gather, eager for a fight. It was 1148. If I lost time here, it would knock off my whole schedule. Just because I had all the time in the world didn't mean I had time to waste. Every hour lost meant I was an hour weaker, and it would catch up with me on the battlefield.

"You runnin', chickenshit?" His voice rang through the cafeteria.

Rita turned and glared at me. It was obvious she had just realized that the recruit who'd been staring at her during PT was eating in the same cafeteria. Something told me that if I returned her gaze, she'd help me the way she'd helped during PT—the way she'd helped in my first battle. Rita wasn't the type who could turn her back on someone in trouble. Her humanity was starting to show through. I wondered what her play would be. Maybe she'd start talking about green tea to cool this guy off. I laughed under my breath at the thought.

"What's so funny?"

Oops. "Nothing to do with you."

My eyes left Rita. The Keiji Kiriya standing in the cafeteria that day was no green recruit. My outward appearance may have been the same, but inside I was a hardened veteran of seventy-nine battles. I could deal with my own problems. I'd imposed on Rita once during PT and once more, indirectly, by smooth-talking my way into one of her spare battle axes. I didn't need to involve her a third time just to make it through lunch.

"You fuckin' with me?" He wasn't going to let this go.

"I'm sorry, but I really don't have time to waste screwing around."

"Whaddayou have hangin' between your legs? A pair of ping pong balls?"

"I never opened my sack to look. You?"

"Motherfucker!"

"That's enough!" A sultry voice cut short our argument. It wasn't Rita.

Salvation had come from an unexpected quarter. I turned to see a bronze-skinned woman standing beside the table. Her apron-bound breasts intruded rudely on a good 60 percent of my field of view. She stood between us holding a steaming fried shrimp with a pair of long cooking chopsticks. It was Rachel Kisaragi.

"I don't want any fighting in here. This is a dining room, not a boxing ring."

"Just tryin' to teach this recruit some manners."

"Well, school's over."

"Hey, you were the one complaining about how miserable he looked eating your food."

"Even so."

Rachel glanced at me. She hadn't shown the slightest hint of anger when I'd knocked over her cart of potatoes, so for this to have gotten to her, I must've been making quite the impression. A part of her probably wanted to embarrass anyone associated with Jin Yonabaru, widely regarded as the most annoying person on base. Not that I blamed her. I'd tripped the spilled potato flag, and now I'd tripped this one. The aftermath was my responsibility.

In a base dyed in coffee-stain splotches of desert earth tones, a woman like Rachel was bound to attract an admirer or two, but I'd never realized just how popular she was. This man hadn't picked a fight with me over some company rivalry. He was showing off.

"It's all right. I shouldn't have said anything." Rachel turned to face the looming giant and shooed me away with a gesture from behind her back. "Here. Have a shrimp. On the house."

"Save it for the penguins."

Rachel frowned.

"Doesn't this runt have anything to say for himself?" He reached one big, meaty arm over Rachel's shoulder and threw a jab.

I reacted instinctively. Subjective months in a Jacket had conditioned me to always keep my feet planted firmly on the ground. My right leg pivoted clockwise, my left counterclockwise, bringing me down into a battle stance. I parried his lunge with my left arm and raised the lunch tray in my right hand to keep the plates from falling, my center of gravity never leaving the middle of my body. Rachel dropped the fried shrimp. I snatched it from its graceful swim through the air before its tail could touch the ground.

The parry had thrown the guy off balance. He took two tottering steps forward, then a third, before tumbling into the lunch of the soldier sitting in front of him. Food and plates went flying with a spectacular crash. I stood, balancing my tray in one hand.

"You dropped this." I handed Rachel the fried shrimp. The onlookers broke into applause.

"Fucking piece of shit!" The guy was up already, his fist flying toward me. He was stubborn. I had a few moments to consider whether I should dodge his punch, launch a counterattack of my own, or turn tail and run.

Speaking from experience, a straight right from a man who'd been trained to pilot a Jacket definitely had some bite, but it didn't register compared to what a Mimic could do. This loser's punch would be strong enough to inflict pain, but not a mortal wound, unless he got extremely lucky. I watched as he put every ounce of his strength into the swing. His fist went sailing right past the tip of my nose. He was neglecting his footwork, leaving an opening. I didn't take it.

There went my first chance to kill you.

He recovered from the missed punch, his breath roaring in his nose. He started hopping around like a boxer. "Stop duckin' and fight like a man, bitch!"

Still haven't had enough?

The gap between our levels of skill was deeper than the Mariana Trench, but I guess that demonstration hadn't been enough for it to sink in. Poor bastard.

He came with a left hook. I moved back half a step.

Whoosh.

Another jab. I stepped back. I could have killed him twice now. There, my third chance. Now a fourth. He was leaving too many openings to count. I could have laid him out on the floor ten times over in a single minute. Lucky for him my job wasn't sending able-bodied Jacket jockeys to the infirmary, no matter how hotheaded they were. My job was sending Mimics to their own private part of Hell.

With each punch he threw and missed, the crowd cried out.

"Come on, you haven't even scratched 'im!"

"Stop prancin' around and take a hit already!"

"Punch him! Punch him! Punch him!"

"Watch the doors, don't want nobody breakin' this up! I got ten bucks on the big one!" Followed immediately by, "Twenty on the scrawny guy!" Hey, that's me! I thought as I dodged another punch. Then someone else cried out, "Where's my fried shrimp? I lost my fried shrimp!"

The wilder the crowd grew, the more effort he put behind his punches and the easier they were to avoid.

Ferrell had a saying: "Break down every second." The first time I heard it, I didn't understand what it meant. A second was a second. There wasn't anything to stretch or break down.

But it turns out that you *can* carve the perception of time into finer and finer pieces. If you flipped a switch in the back of your brain, you could watch a second go by like the frames of a movie. Once you figured out what would be happening ten frames later, you could take whatever steps you needed to turn the situation to your advantage. All at a subconscious level. In battle, you couldn't count on anyone who didn't understand how to break down time.

Evading his attacks was easy. But I didn't want to trip any more unnecessary flags than I already had. I'd gone to a lot of trouble to shift my schedule, but if I kept this up the 17th would be in the cafeteria soon. I needed to bring this diversion to a close before they showed up.

I decided that taking one of his punches would waste the least amount of time. What I didn't count on was Rachel stepping in to try to stop him. She altered the course of his right punch just enough to change the hit that was supposed to glance off my cheek into one that landed square on my chin. A wave of heat spread from my teeth to the back of my nose. The dishes on my tray danced through the air. And there was Rita at the edge of my field of vision, leaving the cafeteria. I would make this pain a lesson for next time. I lost consciousness and wandered through muddy sleep . . .

When I came to, I found myself laid out across several pipe chairs pushed together into a makeshift bed. Something damp was on my head—a woman's handkerchief. A faint citrus smell hung in the air.

"Are you awake?"

I was in the kitchen. Above me an industrial ventilator hummed, siphoning steam from the room. Nearby, an olive green liquid simmered in an enormous pot like the cauldrons angry natives were supposed to use for boiling explorers up to their pith hats, except much larger. Next week's menu hung on the wall. Above the handwritten menu was the head of a man torn from a poster.

After staring at his bleached white teeth for what seemed an eternity, I finally recognized it. It was the head of the body builder from the poster in our barracks. I wondered how he had made it all the way from the men's barracks to his new wall, where he could spend his days smiling knowingly over the women who worked in the kitchen.

Rachel was peeling potatoes, tossing each spiral skin into an oversized basket that matched the scale of the pot. These were the same potatoes that had come raining down on my head my fourth time through the loop. I'd eaten the goddamned mashed potatoes she was making seventy-nine times now. There weren't any other workers in the kitchen aside from Rachel. She must have prepared the meals for all these men on her own.

Sitting up, I bit down on the air a few times to test my jaw. That punch had caught me at just the right angle. Things didn't seem to be lining up the way they should. Rachel caught sight of me.

"Sorry about that. He's really not such a bad guy."

"I know."

She smiled. "You're more mature than you look."

"Not mature enough to stay out of trouble, apparently," I replied with a shrug.

People were always a little high-strung the day before a battle.

And guys were always looking for an opportunity to look good in front of a knockout like Rachel. The deck was definitely stacked against me, though I'm sure the face I'd been making hadn't helped the situation any.

"What are you, a pacifist? Rare breed in these parts."

"I like to save it for the battlefield."

"That explains it."

"Explains what?"

"Why you were holding back. You're obviously the better fighter." Rachel's eyes stared down at me intently. She was tall for a woman. Flower Line Base had been built three years ago. If she'd come to the base immediately after getting her nutritionist's license, that would make her at least four years older than me. But she sure didn't look it. And it wasn't that she went out of her way to make herself look young. The glow of her bronze skin and her warm smile were as natural as they came. She reminded me of the librarian I'd fallen for in high school. The same smile that had stolen my heart and sent me happily to work airing out the library that hot summer so long ago.

"Our lives should be written in stone. Paper is too temporary— too easy to rewrite." Thoughts like that had been on my mind a lot lately.

"That's an odd thing to say."

"Maybe."

"You seeing anyone?"

I looked at her. Green eyes. "No."

"I'm free tonight." Then she added hastily, "Don't get the wrong idea. I don't say that sort of thing to just anyone."

That much I knew. She'd brushed Yonabaru aside readily enough. For an entire week I'd heard complaint after complaint about the hottest woman whose knees were locked together with the biggest padlock. "It's a travesty in this day and age," he'd tell me. And I had a feeling it wasn't special treatment just because Yonabaru was who he was.

"What time is it?" I still had a schedule to keep.

"Almost three o'clock. You were out for about three hours."

1500. I was supposed to be training with Ferrell. I had to make right what I'd done in the last loop—the move that had killed Ferrell and the lieutenant. They'd died protecting me because I was showboating. I could still see the charred, smoldering family pictures Ferrell had decorated the inside of his Jacket with fluttering in the wind. A shot of him smiling under a bright Brazilian sun surrounded by brothers and sisters burned into my mind.

I didn't possess any extraordinary talents that set me apart from my peers. I was just a soldier. There were things I could do, and things I couldn't. If I practiced, in time I could change some of those things I couldn't do into things I could. I wouldn't let my overconfidence kill the people who'd saved my life time and time again.

Under other circumstances I might have accepted her invitation.

"Sorry, but I'm not the guy you're looking for."

I turned and started running toward the training field where Sergeant Ferrell was waiting, reeking of sweat and pumped with adrenaline.

"Asshole!"

I didn't stop to return the compliment.

4

Attempt #99:
  KIA forty-five minutes from start of battle.

5

Attempt #110:
  They break through our line. Yonabaru is the weak link.
  "Keiji . . . that mystery novel. It was that guy eating the pud-
ding who . . ."
  With those words, he dies.
  KIA fifty-seven minutes from start of battle.

6

Attempt #123:
  The migraines that had started after about fifty loops are getting
worse. I don't know what's causing them. The painkillers the doctors give me don't work at all. The prospect of these headaches
accompanying me into every battle from here on out isn't doing
much for my morale.
  KIA sixty-one minutes from start of battle.

7

Attempt #154:

Lose consciousness eighty minutes from start of battle. I don't die, but I'm still caught in the loop.

Whatever.

If that's how it's gonna be, that's how it's gonna be.

8

Attempt #158:

I've finally mastered the tungsten carbide battle axe. I can rip through a Mimic's endoskeleton with a flick of the wrist.

To defeat resilient foes, mankind developed blades that vibrate at ultra-high frequencies, pile drivers that fire spikes at velocities of fifteen hundred meters per second, and explosive melee weapons that utilized the Monroe Effect. But projectile weapons ran out of ammo. They jammed. They broke down. If you struck a slender blade at the wrong angle, it would shatter. And so Rita Vrataski reintroduced war to the simple, yet highly effective, axe.

It was an elegant solution. Every last kilogram-meter per second of momentum generated by the Jacket's actuators was converted to pure destructive force. The axe might bend or chip, but its utility as a weapon would be undiminished. In battle, weapons you could use to bludgeon your enemy were more reliable. Weapons that had been honed to a fine edge, such as the katana, would cut so deep they'd get wedged in your enemy's body and you couldn't pull them out. There were even stories of warriors who dulled their blades with a stone before battle to prevent that from happening. Rita's axe had proven its worth time and again.

My platoon crawled toward the northern tip of Kotoiushi Island, Jackets in sleep mode. It was five minutes before our platoon commander would give the signal for the start of the battle. No matter how many times I experienced it, this was when my tension ran highest. I could see why Yonabaru let his mouth run with whatever bullshit came out. Ferrell just let our chatter wash over him.

"I'm tellin' ya, you gotta hook yourself up with some pussy. If you wait until you're strapped into one of these Jackets, it's too late."

"Yeah."

"What about Mad Wargarita? Y'all were talkin' during PT, right? You'd tap that, I know you would."

"Yeah."

"You're a cool customer."

"Yeah?"

"You haven't even popped your cherry, and you're calm as a fuckin' whore. My first time I had butterflies beatin' up a tornado in my stomach."

"It's like a standardized test."

"What're you talkin' about?"

"Didn't you take those in high school?"

"Dude, you don't expect me to remember high school, do ya?"

"Yeah." I'd managed to throw Yonabaru off what passed for his train of thought, but my mind was on autopilot. "Yeah."

"Yeah what? I didn't even say anything." Yonabaru's voice reached me through a fog.

I felt like I'd been fighting in this same spot for a hundred years. Half a year ago I was a kid in high school. I couldn't have cared less about a war that was slowly drowning the earth in its own blood. I'd lived in a world of peace, one filled with family and

friends. I never imagined I'd trade classrooms and the soccer field
for a war zone.

"You've been actin' funny since yesterday."

"Yeah?"

"Dude, don't go losin' it on us. Two in a row from the same
platoon—how would that look? And I been meanin' to ask: what
the fuck is that hunk of metal you're carrying? And what the fuck
do you plan on doin' with it? Tryin' to assert your ind'viduality?
Workin' on an art project?"

"It's for crushing."

"Crushin' what?"

"The enemy, mostly."

"You get up close, that's what your pile driver's for. You gonna
tell me you're better off with an axe? Maybe we should fill our
platoon with lumberjacks. Hi ho, hi ho!"

"That was the dwarves."

"Good point. Well made. Point for you."

Ferrell jumped into our conversation. "Hey, I don't know where
he learned how, but he sure as hell can use that thing. But Kiriya,
only use it once they're up in your face and you don't have a choice.
Don't go rushin' up askin' for it. Modern warfare is still waged with
bullets. Try not to forget."

"Yessir."

"Yonabaru."

I guess the sergeant felt he needed to spread the attention
around.

"Yeah?"

"Just . . . do what you always do."

"What the hell, Sarge? Keiji gets a pep talk and I get that? A
delicate soul like me needs some inspiring words of encourage-
ment, too."

"I might as well encourage my rifle for all the good it would
do."

"You know what this is? Discrimination, that's what it is!"

"Every now and again you get me thinking, Yonabaru," Ferrell said, his voice tinny over the link. "I'd give my pension to the man who invents a way to fasten your—shit, it's started! Don't get your balls blown off, gents!"

I sprang into battle, Doppler cranked, the usual buzzing in my helmet. Just like the other moments.

There. A target.

I fired. I ducked. A javelin whizzed past my head.

"Who's up there? You're too far forward! You wanna get yourself killed?"

I pretended to follow the platoon leader's orders. I don't care how many lives you have, if you followed the orders of every officer fresh from the academy, you'd end up getting bored of dying.

Thunder erupted from the shells crisscrossing the sky. I wiped sand from my helmet. I glanced at Ferrell and nodded. It only took an instant for him to realize the suppressing fire I'd just laid down had thwarted an enemy ambush. Somewhere deep in Ferrell's gut, his instincts were telling him that this recruit named Keiji Kiriya, who'd never set foot in battle in his life, was a soldier he could use. He was able to see past the recklessness of what I'd just done. It was that sort of adaptability that had kept him alive for twenty years.

To be honest, Ferrell was the only man in the platoon *I* could use. The other soldiers had only seen two or three battles at most. Even the ones who'd survived in the past hadn't ever gotten killed. You can't learn from your mistakes when they kill you. These greenhorns didn't know what it was to walk the razor's edge between life and death. They didn't know that the line dividing the two, the borderland piled high with corpses, was the easiest place to survive. The fear that permeated every fiber of my being was relentless, it was cruel, and it was my best hope for getting through this.

That was the only way to fight the Mimics. I didn't know shit about any other wars, and frankly, I didn't care to. My enemy was humanity's enemy. The rest didn't matter.

The fear never left me. My body trembled with it. When I sensed the presence of an enemy just outside my field of vision, I could feel it crawling along my spine. Who had told me that fear had a way of seeping into your body? Had it been the platoon leader? Or was it Ferrell? Maybe it was something I'd heard during training.

But even as the fear racks my body, it soothes me, comforts me. Soldiers who get washed away in a rush of adrenaline don't survive. In war, fear is the woman your mother warned you about. You knew she was no good for you, but you couldn't shake her. You had to find a way to get along, because she wasn't going anywhere.

The 17th Company of the 3rd Battalion, 12th Regiment, 301st Armored Infantry Division was cannon fodder. If the frontal assault succeeded, the Mimics fleeing the siege would wash over us like a torrent of water surging through a dry gully. If it failed, we'd be a lone platoon in the middle of a sea of hostiles. Either way our odds of survival were slim. The platoon commander knew it, and Sergeant Ferrell knew it. The whole company was pieced together from soldiers who'd survived the slaughter at Okinawa. Who better to give this shit assignment to? In an operation involving twenty-five thousand Jackets, if a lone company of 146 men got wiped out, it wouldn't even rate a memo on the desk of the brass in the Defense Ministry. We were the sacrificial lambs whose blood greased the wheels of war's machinery.

Of course, there were only three kinds of battle to begin with: fucked up, seriously fucked up, and fucked up beyond all recognition. No use panicking about it. There'd be plenty of chaos to go around. Same Jackets. Same enemy. Same buddies. Same me, same muscles that weren't ready for what I was asking of them screaming in protest.

My body never changed, but the OS that ran it had seen a total overhaul. I'd started as a green recruit, a paper doll swept on the winds of war. I'd become a veteran who bent the war to my will. I bore the burden of endless battle like the killing machine I'd become—a machine with blood and nerves in place of oil and wires. A machine doesn't get distracted. A machine doesn't cry. A machine wears the same bitter smile day in, day out. It reads the battle as it unfolds. Its eyes scan for the next enemy before it's finished killing the first, and its mind is already thinking about the third. It wasn't lucky, and it wasn't unlucky. It just was. So I kept fighting. If this was going to go on forever, it would go on forever.

Shoot. Run. Plant one foot, then the other. Keep moving.

A javelin tore through the air I had occupied only a tenth of a second before. It dug into the ground before detonating, blasting dirt and sand into the air. I'd caught a break. The enemy couldn't see through the shower of falling earth—I could. There. One, two, three. I took down the Mimics through the improvised curtain of dust.

I accidentally kicked one of my buddies—the sort of kick you used to break down a door when both of your hands were full. I had a gun in my left hand and a battle axe in my right. It was a good thing God had given us two arms and legs. If I only had three appendages to work with, I wouldn't be able to help this soldier out, whoever he was.

As I turned, I cut down another Mimic with a single blow. I ran up to the fallen soldier. He had a wolf wearing a crown painted on his armor—4th Company. If they were here, that meant we'd met up with the main assault force. The line was giving way.

The soldier's shoulders were trembling. He was in shock. Whether it was the Mimics or my kick that had sent him into it, I couldn't tell. He was oblivious to the world around him. If I left him there, he'd be a corpse inside of three minutes.

I put my hand on his shoulder plate and established a contact comm.

"You remember how many points we beat you by in that game?"

He didn't answer. "You know, the one you lost to 17th Company."

"Wh . . . what?" The words rasped in his throat.

"The rugby game. Don't you remember? It was some kind of intramural record, so I figure we musta beat you by at least ten, twenty points."

I realized what I was doing.

"You know, it's funny, me talkin' to you like this. Hey, you don't think she'd charge me for stealin' her idea, do you? It's not like she has a patent on it or anything."

"What? What are you talkin' about?"

"You'll be fine." He was snapping out of it pretty quick—he was no rookie like I'd been. I slapped him on the back. "You owe me, 4th Company. What's your name?"

"Kogoro Murata, and I don't owe you shit."

"Keiji Kiriya."

"That's some attitude you got. Not sure I like it."

"The feeling's mutual. Let's hope our luck holds."

We bumped fists and parted ways.

I swept my head from left to right. I ran. I pulled my trigger. My body had long since passed exhaustion, but a part of me maintained a heightened sense of alertness impossible under normal circumstances. My mind was a conveyer belt sorting good apples from the bad—any piece of information that wasn't vital to survival was automatically shut out.

I saw Rita Vrataski. The rumble of an explosion heralded her arrival. A laser-guided bomb fell from a plane circling overhead, far out of reach of the enemy. It covered the distance between us in under twenty seconds, detonating precisely where the Valkyrie had called it down.

Rita was headed for the spot the bomb had struck, a shattered mix of debris, equal parts living and dead. Creatures streamed from the crater toward her swinging battle axe.

Even in the midst of battle, seeing Rita's red Jacket stirred something in me. Her mere presence had breathed new life into our broken line. Her skill was peerless, the product of U.S. Special Forces' efforts to make a soldier to end all soldiers. But it was more than that. She really was our savior.

Just a glimpse of her Jacket on the battlefield would drive soldiers to give another ten percent, even if they didn't have it left to spare. I'm sure there were men who'd see her and fall in love, like a man and a woman on a sinking ship spying one another between waves. Death could come at any moment on the battlefield, so why not? The wise guys who'd named her Full Metal Bitch had really fished around for that one.

I didn't think they had it right. Or maybe I was starting to feel something for Rita Vrataski myself. That suited me fine. Trapped in this fucking loop, I had no hope of falling in love. Even if I found someone who could love me in one short day, she'd be gone the next. The loop robbed me of every moment I spent with someone.

Rita had saved me once, long ago. She had kept me calm with her random talk of green tea. She had told me she'd stay with me until I died. What better target for my unrequited love than our savior herself?

My OS continued to respond automatically, despite the distraction my emotions were giving it. My body twisted. I planted a foot on the ground. I didn't have to think about the battle unfolding before my eyes. Thought only got in the way. Deciding which way to move, and how, were things you did in training. If you paused to think in battle, Death would be there waiting, ready to swing his scythe.

I fought on.

It was seventy-two minutes since the battle had started. Tanaka, Maie, Ube, and Nijou were all KIA. Four dead, seven wounded, and zero missing. Nijou had hung the poster of the swimsuit model on the wall. Maie was from somewhere deep inside China. He never said a word. I didn't know much about the other two. I etched the faces of the men I'd let die deep in my mind. In a few hours their pain would be gone, but I would remember. Like a thorn in my heart it tormented me, toughened me for the next battle.

Somehow our platoon had held together. I could hear the blades of the choppers in the distance. They hadn't been shot out of the sky. This was the best attempt yet. The platoon leader had no words for the recruit who'd taken matters into his own hands. Every now and then Ferrell would fire a few rounds my way to help out.

And then I saw it—the Mimic I'd fought in the first battle that had trapped me in this fucking loop. I'd fired three pile driver rounds into it that day. I don't know how, but I knew it was the one. On the outside it was the same bloated frog corpse as all the rest, but here on my 157th pass through the loop, I could still recognize the Mimic that had killed me the first time.

It had to die with extreme prejudice.

Somehow I knew that if I could kill it, I'd pass some sort of boundary. It may not break this loop of battle after battle after battle, but *something* would change, however small. I was sure of it.

Stay right there. I'm comin' for ya.

Speaking of crossing boundaries, I still hadn't read any further in that mystery novel. I don't know why that occurred to me then, but it did. I'd spent some of my last precious hours reading that book. I'd stopped just as the detective was about to reveal who done it. I'd been so preoccupied with training I hadn't given it another thought. It must have been nearly a year now. Maybe it was time I got around to finishing that book. If I killed this Mimic and made it to the next level, I'd start on that last chapter.

I readied my battle axe. Caution to the wind, I charged.

Static crackled in my headphones. Someone was talking to me. A woman. It was our savior, the Full Metal Bitch, Valkyrie reborn, Mad Wargarita—Rita Vrataski.

"How many loops is this for you?"

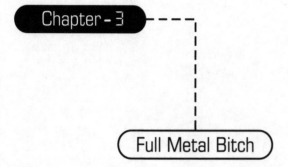

Chapter - 3

Full Metal Bitch

1

A brilliant sun traced crisp shadows on the ground. The air was so clean you could have gotten a clear sniper shot from kilometers away. Above the field, the 17th Company's flag snapped in a moist southerly breeze blowing off the Pacific.

The sea air held a scent that snaked its way down your nose and tickled your tongue on its way to your throat. Rita knitted her brow. It wasn't the stench of a Mimic. More like the slightly fishy fragrance you got from those bowls of nuoc mam sauce.

Wartime tensions and the constant threat of death aside, the Far East really wasn't so bad. The coastline, so difficult to defend, afforded beautiful sunsets. The air and water were clean. If Rita, who had about one tenth the refinement and culture of an average individual, thought it was wonderful here, an actual tourist might have considered it paradise. If there were one mark against it, it was the cloying humidity.

The weather that night would be perfect for an air strike. Once the sun had set, bombers laden with GPS-guided munitions would take to the sky in swarms to blast the island into a lifeless moonscape before the next morning's ground assault. The beautiful atoll and the flora and fauna that called it home would all share the same fate as the enemy, if everything went according to plan.

"Beautiful day, don't you think, Major Vrataski?" An old film camera dangled from the man's thick neck, a redwood trunk by comparison to the average Jacket jockey's beech-tree. Rita casually ignored him.

"Great lighting. Days like today can make even a steel-and-rivets airplane look like a da Vinci."

Rita snorted. "You doing fine art photography now?"

"That's hardly any way to speak to the only embedded photojournalist in the Japan expedition. I take great pride in the role I play conveying the truths of this war to the public. Of course, 90 percent of the truth is lighting."

"Pretty slick talk. They must love you over at PR. How many tongues you figure you have?"

"Only the one the Lord saw fit to bestow Americans with. Though I hear Russians and Cretans have two."

"Well I hear there's a Japanese god who pulls out the tongues of liars. Don't do anything to get yours in trouble."

"Perish the thought."

The corner of the training field Rita and the photographer were standing on caught the full force of the wind coming off the ocean. In the middle of the giant field, 146 men from the 17th Company of the 301st Japanese Armored Infantry Division were frozen in neat rows along the ground. It was a kind of training called iso push-ups. Rita hadn't seen it before.

The rest of Rita's squad stood a short distance away, their thick, bristly arms jutting out before them. They were busy doing what soldiers did best, which was mocking those less fortunate than themselves. *Maybe this is how they practice bowing? Hey, samurai! Try picking up a sword after an hour of that!*

None of Rita's squadmates would go near her within thirty hours of an attack. It was an unspoken rule. The only people who dared approach her were a Native American engineer who couldn't hardly see straight and the photographer, Ralph Murdoch.

"They don't move at all?" Rita seemed doubtful.

"No, they just hold that position."

"I don't know if I'd call it samurai training. Looks more like yoga if you ask me."

"Is it odd to find similarities between Indian mysticism and Japanese tradition?"

"Ninety-eight!"

"Ninety-eight!"

"Ninety-nine!"

"Ninety-nine!"

Staring into the ground like farmers watching rice grow, the soldiers barked in time with the drill sergeant. The shouts of the 146 men echoed in Rita's skull. A familiar migraine sent wires of pain through her head. This was a bad one.

"Another headache?"

"None of your business."

"I don't see how a platoon worth of doctors can't find a cure for one headache."

"Neither do I. Why don't you try to find out?" she snapped.

"They keep those guys on a pretty short leash. I can't even get an interview."

Murdoch raised his camera. It wasn't clear what he intended to do with the images of the spectacle unfolding in perfect stillness before him. Maybe sell them to a tabloid with nothing better to print.

"I'm not sure that's in very good taste." Rita didn't know a single soldier on the field, but she didn't have to know them to like them better than Murdoch.

"Pictures are neither tasteful nor distasteful. If you click on a link and a picture of a corpse pops up, you might have grounds for a lawsuit. If that same picture appears on the homepage of the *New York Times*, it could win a Pulitzer Prize."

"This is different."

"Is it?"

"You're the one who broke into the data processing center. If it weren't for your slip-up, these men wouldn't be here being punished, and you wouldn't be here taking pictures of them. I'd say that qualifies as distasteful."

"Not so fast. I've been wrongly accused." The sound of his camera shutter grew more frequent, masking their conversation.

"Security here is lax compared to central command. I don't know what you were trying to dig up out here in the boondocks, but don't hurt anyone else doing it."

"So you're onto me."

"I'd just hate to see the censors come down on you right when you land your big scoop."

"The government can tell us any truths they please. But there are truths, and there are *truths*," Murdoch said. "It's up to the people to decide which is which. Even if it's something the government doesn't want reported."

"How egotistical."

"Name a good journalist who isn't. You have to be to find a story. Do you know any Dreamers?"

"I'm not interested in feed religions."

"Did you know the Mimics went on the move at almost exactly the same time you started that big operation up in Florida?"

The Dreamers were a pacifist group—civilian, of course. The emergence of the Mimics had had a tremendous impact on marine ecosystems. Organizations that had called for the protection of dolphins, whales, and other marine mammals died out. The Dreamers picked up where they left off.

Dreamers believed the Mimics were intelligent, and they insisted it was humanity's failure to communicate with them that had led to this war. They reasoned that if Mimics could evolve so quickly into such potent weapons, with patience, they could develop the means to communicate as well. The Dreamers had begun to take in members of a war-weary public who believed humanity could never triumph over the Mimics, and in the past two to three years the size of the movement had ballooned.

"I interviewed a few before coming to Japan," Murdoch continued.

"Sounds like hard work."

"They all have the same dream on the same day. In that dream, humanity falls to the Mimics. They think it's some sort of message they're trying to send us. Not that you needed me to tell you that." Murdoch licked his lips. His tongue was too small for his body, giving the distinct impression of a mollusk. "I did a little digging, and it turns out there are particularly high concentrations of these dreams in the days before U.S. Spec Ops launch major attacks. And over the past few years, more and more people have been having the dream. It hasn't been made public, but some of these people are even in the military."

"You believe whatever these feed jobs tell you? Listen to them long enough and they'd have you thinking sea monkeys were regular Einsteins."

"Academic circles are already discussing the possibility of Mimic intelligence. And if they are, it's not far-fetched to think they would try to communicate."

"You shouldn't assume everything you don't understand is a message," Rita said. She snorted. "Keep on like that, and next thing you'll be telling me you've found signs of intelligence in our government, and we both know that's never going to happen."

"Very funny. But there's a science here you can't ignore. Each step up the evolutionary ladder—from single-celled organism, to cold-blooded animal, to warm-blooded animal—has seen a tenfold increase in energy consumption." Ralph licked his lips again. "If you look at the amount of energy a human in modern society consumes, it's ten times greater than that of a warm-blooded animal of similar size. Yet Mimics, which are supposed to be a cold-blooded animal, consume the same amount of energy as humans."

"That supposed to mean they're higher than us on the ladder? That's quite a theory. You should have it published."

"I seem to recall you saying something about having dreams."

"Sure I have dreams. Ordinary dreams."

To Rita, looking for meaning in dreams was a waste of time. A nightmare was a nightmare. And the time loops she'd stumbled into in the course of the war, well, they were something else entirely. "We have an attack coming up tomorrow. Did any of the people you interviewed get a message?"

"Absolutely. I called L.A. this morning to confirm it. All three had had the dream."

"Now I know it's not true. That's impossible."

"How would you know?"

"This is only the first time through today."

"That again? How can a day have a first time or a second time?"

"Just hope you never find out."

Murdoch made a show of shrugging. Rita returned her gaze to the unlucky men on the field.

Jacket jockeys didn't have much use for muscle. Endurance was the order of the day, not stamina-draining burst power. To build their endurance, Rita's squad practiced a standing technique from kung fu known as *ma bu*. Ma bu consisted of spreading your legs as though you were straddling a horse and maintaining the position for an extended period of time. In addition to strengthening leg muscle, it was an extremely effective way to improve balance.

Rita wasn't sure what benefit, if any, the iso push-ups were supposed to have. It looked more like punishment, plain and simple. The Japanese soldiers, packed together like sardines in a can, remained frozen in that one position. For them, this probably ranked among the worst experiences of their lives. Even so, Rita envied them this simple memory. Rita hadn't shared that sort of throwaway experience with anyone in a long time.

The stifling wind tugged at her rust-red hair. Her bangs, still too long no matter how many times she cut them, made her forehead itch.

This was the world as it was at the start of the loop. What happened here only Rita would remember. The sweat of the Japanese soldiers, the whoops and jeers of the U.S. Special Forces—it would all be gone without a trace.

Maybe it would have been best not to think about it, but watching these soldiers training the day before an attack, sweat-soaked shirts sticking to their skin in the damp air, she felt sorry for them. In a way, this was her fault for bringing Murdoch along with her.

Rita decided to find a way to shorten the PT and put an end to this seemingly pointless exercise. So what if it instilled a samurai fighting spirit? They'd still wet themselves the first time they ran into a Mimic assault. She wanted to stop it, even if it was a sentimental gesture that no one but herself would ever appreciate.

Surveying the training field, Rita chanced upon a pair of defiant eyes staring directly at her. She was accustomed to being looked on with awe, admiration, even fear, but she'd never seen this: a

look filled with such unbridled hatred from a complete stranger.
If a person could shoot lasers from their eyes, Rita would have
been baked crisper than a Thanksgiving turkey in about three
seconds.

She had only met one other man whose eyes even approached
the same intensity. Arthur Hendricks's deep blue eyes had known
no fear. Rita had killed him, and now those blue eyes were buried
deep in the cold earth.

Judging by his muscles, the soldier staring at her was a rookie
not long out of boot camp. Nothing like Hendricks. He had been
an American, a lieutenant, and the commander of the U.S. Special
Forces squad.

The color of this soldier's eyes was different. His hair, too. His
face and body weren't even close. Still, there was something about
this Asian soldier that Rita Vrataski liked.

2

Rita had often wondered what the world would be like if there
were a machine that could definitively measure the sum of a person's potential.

If DNA determined a person's height or the shape of their face,
why not their less obvious traits too? Our fathers and mothers,
grandfathers and grandmothers—ultimately every individual was
the product of the blood that flowed in the veins of those who came
before. An impartial machine could read that information and assign
a value to it, as simple as measuring height or weight.

What if someone who had the potential to discover a formula
to unlock the mysteries of the universe wanted to become a pulp
fiction writer? What if someone who had the potential to create
unparalleled gastronomic delicacies had his heart set on civil engi-

neering? There is what we desire to do, and what we are able to do. When those two things don't coincide, which path should we pursue to find happiness?

When Rita was young, she had a gift for two things: playing horseshoes and pretending to cry. The thought that her DNA contained the potential to become a great warrior couldn't have been further from her mind.

Before she lost her parents when she was fifteen, she was an ordinary kid who didn't like her carrot-top hair. She wasn't particularly good at sports, and her grades in junior high school were average. There was nothing about her dislike of bell peppers and celery that set her apart. Only her ability to feign crying was truly exceptional. She couldn't fool her mother, whose eagle eyes saw through her every ruse, but with anyone else she'd have them eating out of her hand after a few seconds of waterworks. Rita's only other distinguishing feature was the red hair she'd inherited from her grandmother. Everything else about her was exactly like any other of over three hundred million Americans.

Her family lived in Pittsfield, a small town just east of the Mississippi River. Not the Pittsfield in Florida, not the Pittsfield in Massachusetts, but the Pittsfield in Illinois. Her father was the youngest child in a family of martial artists—mostly jujutsu. But Rita didn't want to go to a military academy or play sports. She wanted to stay at home and raise pigs.

With the exception of the young men who signed up with the UDF, life for the people of Pittsfield was peaceful. It was an easy place to forget that humanity was in the middle of a war against a strange and terrible foe.

Rita didn't mind living in a small town and never seeing anyone but the same four thousand people or so. Listening to the squeals of the pigs day in and day out could get a little tiresome, but the air was clean and the sky wide. She always had a secret spot where she could go to daydream and look for four-leaf clovers.

An old retired trader had a small general store in town. He sold everything from foodstuffs and hardware to little silver crosses that were supposed to keep the Mimics away. He carried all-natural coffee beans you couldn't find anyplace else.

The Mimic attacks had turned most of the arable land in developing countries to desert, leaving luxury foods like natural coffee, tea, and tobacco extremely difficult to come by. They'd been replaced with substitutes or artificially flavored tastealikes that usually failed.

Rita's town was one of many attempting to provide the produce and livestock needed by a hungry nation and its army.

The first victims of the Mimic attacks were also the most vulnerable: the poorest regions of Africa and South America. The archipelagos of Southeast Asia. Countries that lacked the means to defend themselves watched as the encroaching desert devoured their land. People abandoned the cultivation of cash crops—the coffee, tea, tobacco, and spices coveted in wealthier nations—and began growing staples, beans and sorghum, anything to stave off starvation. Developed nations had generally been able to stop the Mimic advance at the coastline, but much of the produce they had taken for granted disappeared from markets and store shelves overnight.

Rita's father, who had grown up in a world where even Midwesterners could have fresh sushi every day, was, it is no exaggeration to say, a coffee addict. He didn't smoke or drink—coffee was his vice. Often he would take Rita by the hand and sneak off with her to the old man's store when Rita's mother wasn't watching.

The old man had skin of bronze and a bushy white beard.

When he wasn't telling stories, he chewed the stem of his hookah hose between puffs. He spent his days surrounded by exotic goods from countries most people had never heard of. There were small animals wrought in silver. Grotesque dolls. Totem poles carved with the faces of birds or stranger beasts. The air of the shop was a heady mix of the old man's smoke, untold spices, and all-natural coffee beans still carrying a hint of the rich soil in which they grew.

"These beans are from Chile. These here are from Malawi, in Africa. And these traveled all the way down the Silk Road from Vietnam to Europe," he'd tell Rita. The beans all looked the same to her, but she would point, and the old man would rattle off their pedigrees.

"Got any Tanzanian in today?" Her father was well versed in coffee.

"What, you finish the last batch already?"

"Now you're starting to sound like my wife. What can I say? They're my favorite."

"How about these—now these are really something. Premium Kona coffee grown on the Big Island of Hawaii. Seldom find these even in New York or Washington. Just smell that aroma!"

The wrinkles on the old man's head deepened into creases as he smiled. Rita's father crossed his arms, clearly impressed. He was enjoying this difficult dilemma. The countertop was slightly higher than Rita's head, so she had to stand on tiptoe to get a good look.

"They got Hawaii. I saw it on TV."

"You're certainly well informed, young lady."

"You shouldn't make fun. Kids watch way more news than grown-ups do. All they care about is baseball and football."

"You're certainly right about that." The old man stroked his forehead. "Yes, this is the last of it. The last Kona coffee on the face of the earth. Once it's gone, it's gone."

"Where'd you get ahold of something like that?"

"That, my dear, is a secret."

The hempen bag was packed with cream-colored beans. They were slightly more round than most coffee beans, but they looked ordinary in all other respects.

Rita picked up one of the beans and inspected it. The unroasted specimen was cool and pleasant to the touch. She imagined the beans basking in the sun of an azure sky that spread all the way to the horizon. Her father had told her about the skies over the islands. Rita didn't mind that the skies in Pittsfield were a thin and watery blue, but just once she wanted to see the skies that had filled those beans with the warmth of the sun.

"Do you like coffee, young lady?"

"Not really. It's not sweet. I prefer chocolate."

"Pity."

"It smells nice, though. And these ones definitely smell best of all," Rita said.

"Ah, then there's hope for you yet. What do you say, care to take over my shop when I retire?"

Rita's father, who until then hadn't looked up from the coffee beans, interrupted. "Don't put any ideas in her head. We need someone to carry on the farm, and she's all we've got."

"Then maybe she can find a promising young boy or girl for me to pass on my shop to, eh?"

"I don't know, I'll think about it," Rita answered with indifference.

Her father set down the bag of coffee he'd been admiring and kneeled to look Rita in the eye.

"I thought you wanted to help out on the farm?"

The old man hastily interjected, "Let the child make up her own mind. It's still a free country."

A light flared in the young Rita's eyes. "That's right, Dad. I get to choose, right? Well, as long as they don't make me join the army."

"Don't like the army either, eh? The UDF isn't all bad, you know."

Rita's father scowled. "This is my daughter you're talking to."

"But anyone can enlist once they turn eighteen. We all have the right to defend our country, son and daughter alike. It's quite the opportunity."

"I'm just not sure I want my daughter in the military."

"Well I don't wanna join the army in the first place, Dad."

"Oh, why's that?" A look of genuine curiosity crossed the old man's face.

"You can't eat Mimics. I read so in a book. And you shouldn't kill animals you can't eat just for the sake of killing them. Our teachers and our pastor and everyone says so."

"You're going to be quite a handful when you grow up, aren't you."

"I just wanna be like everybody else."

Rita's father and the old man looked at each other and shared a knowing chuckle. Rita didn't understand what was so funny.

Four years later, the Mimics would attack Pittsfield. The raid came in the middle of an unusually harsh winter. Snow fell faster than it could be cleared from the streets. The city was frozen to a halt.

No one knew this at the time, but Mimics send out something akin to a scouting party before an attack, a small, fast-moving group whose purpose is to advance as far as possible then return with information for the others. That January, three Mimics had slipped past the UDF quarantine and made their way up the Mississippi River undetected.

If the townspeople hadn't noticed something suspicious moving in the shadows, it's doubtful the scouting party would have taken particular notice of Pittsfield, with its livestock and acres of farmland. As it turned out, the shot fired from the hunting rifle of the night watch led to a massacre.

The state guard was immobilized by the snow. It would be hours before a UDF platoon could be lifted in by helicopter. By then, half the buildings in town had burnt to the ground and one out of three of the town's fifteen hundred residents had been killed. The mayor, the preacher, and the old man from the general store were among the dead.

Men who had chosen to grow corn rather than join the army died fighting to defend their families. Small arms were no use against Mimics. Bullets only glanced off their bodies. Mimic javelins ripped through the walls of wooden and even brick houses with ease.

In the end, a ragged bunch of townspeople defeated the three Mimics with their bare hands. They waited until the Mimics were about to fire before rushing them, knocking the creatures into each others' javelins. They killed two of the Mimics this way, and drove off the third.

Dying, Rita's mother sheltered her daughter in her arms. Rita watched in the snow as her father fought and was killed. Smoke spiraled up from the flames. Brilliant cinders flitted up into the night. The sky glowed blood red.

From beneath her mother's body, already beginning to grow cold, Rita considered. Her mother, a devout Christian, had told her that pretending to cry was a lie, and that if she lied, when God judged her immortal soul she wouldn't be allowed into Heaven. When her mother told Rita that if Mimics didn't lie they could get into Heaven, the girl had grown angry. Mimics weren't even from Earth. They didn't have souls, did they? If they did, and they really did go to Heaven, Rita wondered whether people and Mimics would fight up there. Maybe that's what awaited her parents.

The government sent Rita to live with some distant relatives. She stole a passport from a refugee three years older than she who lived in a run-down apartment next door and headed for the UDF recruiting office.

All over the country, people were getting tired of the war. The UDF needed all the soldiers they could get for the front lines.

Provided the applicant hadn't committed a particularly heinous crime, the army wouldn't turn anyone away. Legally, Rita wasn't old enough to enlist, but the recruiting officer barely even glanced at her purloined passport before handing her a contract.

The army granted people one last day to back out of enlistment if they were having second thoughts. Rita, whose last name was now Vrataski, spent her last day on a hard bench outside the UDF office.

Rita didn't have any second thoughts. She only wanted one thing: to kill every last Mimic that had invaded her planet. She knew she could do it. She was her father's daughter.

3

On the next clear night, look up in the direction of the constellation humanity calls Cancer. Between the pincers of the right claw of that giant crab in the sky sits a faint star. No matter how hard you stare, you won't see it with the naked eye. It can only be viewed through a telescope with a thirty-meter aperture. Even if you could travel at the speed of light, fast enough to circle the earth seven and a half times in a single second, it would take over forty years to reach that star. Signals from Earth scatter and disperse on their journey across the vast gulf between.

On a planet revolving around this star lived life in greater numbers and diversity than that on Earth. Cultures more advanced than ours rose and flourished, and creatures with intelligence far surpassing that of *H. sapiens sapiens* held dominion. For the purposes of this fairy tale, we'll call them people.

One day, a person on this planet invented a device called an ecoforming bomb. The device could be affixed to the tip of a spacecraft. This spacecraft, far simpler than any similar craft burdened with life and the means to support it, could cross the void of space with relative ease. Upon reaching its destination, the ship's payload would detonate, showering nanobots over the planet's surface.

Immediately upon arrival, the nanobots would begin to reshape the world, transforming any harsh environment into one suitable for colonization by the people who made them. The actual process is far more complicated, but the details are unimportant. The spacecraft ferrying colonists to the new world would arrive after the nanobots had already completed the transformation.

The scholars among these people questioned whether it was ethical to destroy the existing environment of a planet without first examining it. After all, once done, the process could not be undone. It seemed reasonable to conclude that a planet so readily adapted to support life from their own world might also host indigenous life, perhaps even intelligent life, of its own. Was it right, they asked, to steal a world, sight unseen, from its native inhabitants?

The creators of the device argued that their civilization was built on advancements that could not be undone. To expand their territory, they had never shied away from sacrificing lesser life in the past. Forests had been cleared, swamps drained, dams built. There had been countless examples of people destroying habitats and driving species to extinction for their own benefit. If they could do this on their own planet, why should some unknown world in the void of space be treated differently?

The scholars insisted that the ecoforming of a planet which might harbor intelligent life required direct oversight. Their protests were recorded, considered, and ultimately ignored.

There were concerns more pressing than the preservation of whatever life might be unwittingly stomped out by their ecoforming projects. The people had grown too numerous for their own planet, and so they required another to support their burgeoning population. The chosen world's parent star could not be at too great a distance, nor would a binary or flare star suffice. The planet itself would have to maintain an orbit around a G-class star at a distance sufficient for water to exist in liquid form. The one star system that met these criteria was the star we call the sun. They did not worry for long that this one star might be the only one in this corner of the Milky Way that was home to intelligent life like their own. No attempt was made to communicate. The planet was over forty years away at the speed of light, and there was no time to wait eighty years for the chance of a reply.

The spacecraft built on that distant planet eventually reached Earth. It brought with it no members of their species. No weapons of invasion. It was basically nothing more than a construction machine.

When it was detected, the interstellar craft drew the attention of the world. But all Earth's attempts to make contact went unanswered. Then the ship split into eight pieces. Four of the pieces sank deep under the ocean, while three fell on land. The final piece remained in orbit. The pieces that landed in North Africa and Australia were handed over to NATO. Russia and China fought over the piece that landed in Asia, but China came out on top. After much arguing among the nations of Earth, the orbiting mothership was reduced to a small piece of space junk by a volley of missiles.

The crèche machines that came to rest on the ocean floor began carrying out their instructions quietly and methodically. In the depths, the machines chanced upon echinoderms—starfish. The crèche-produced nanobots penetrated the rigid endoskeletons of the starfish and began to multiply in symbiosis with their hosts.

The resulting creatures fed on soil. They ate the world and shat out poison. What passed through their bodies was toxic to life on Earth, but suitable for the people who had sent them. Slowly, the land where the creatures fed died and became desert. The seas where they spread turned a milky green.

At first it was thought that the creatures were the result of mutations caused by chemical runoff, or perhaps some prehistoric life-form released by tectonic activity. Some scientists insisted it was a species of evolved salamander, though they had no evidence to support their conclusion. Eventually, these new creatures formed groups and began venturing out of the water. They continued their work to reshape the earth with no regard for the society of man.

When they first appeared on land, the alien xenoformers were not weapons of war. They were sluggish, and a group of armed men could easily dispatch them. But like cockroaches that develop resistance to pesticides, the alien creatures evolved. The crèche machines that created them concluded that in order to fulfill their objective of xenoforming the planet, they would have to remove the obstacles standing in their way.

War engulfed the world. The damage wrought was swift and massive. In response, a worldwide United Defense Force was established. Mankind had a name for the enemy that had brought the world to the brink of ruin. We called them Mimics.

4

Rita Vrataski joined U.S. Special Forces after the battle that earned her the Thor's Medal of Valor. The medal, which bears a likeness of said deity brandishing a hammer, is awarded to any soldier who kills ten or more Mimics in a single battle. The Mimics had emerged as the only foe capable of standing against a platoon of fifty armed infantry raining a hail of bullets. Few Thor medals needed to be struck.

The officer who hung the gleaming medal around Rita's neck praised her for joining the elite ranks of those who could claim to have taken down a double handful of Mimics. Rita was the first soldier in history to receive the honor on her second battle. There were some who wondered aloud, to her face, how Rita could have possibly acquired the skills needed to accomplish such a feat by what was only her second field operation. Rita answered them with a question of her own:

"Is cooking dangerous?"

Most would answer no. But what is a gas range but a short-range flame thrower? Any number of flammable materials might lie waiting beneath the average kitchen sink. Shelves lined with pots could weaken and fall in an avalanche of iron and steel. A butcher's knife could kill as easily as a dagger.

Yet few people would consider cooking a dangerous profession, and indeed, the actual danger is remote. Anyone who has spent any time in a kitchen is familiar with the inherent risks, such as they are, and knows what can be done safely and what can't. Never throw water on an oil fire, keep the knife pointed away from your carotid artery, don't use rat poison when the recipe calls for parmesan cheese.

To Rita, war was no different.

The Mimics' attacks were simpleminded. They reminded Rita of the swine she'd raised back in Pittsfield. Soldiers would single out a Mimic to attack, but Mimics did things the other way around. Like a broom sweeping dust off the floor, Mimics attacked entire groups of soldiers at once. As long as you knew how to avoid the broom, no matter how many times the Mimics attacked, you wouldn't get swept away. The secret to fighting the Mimics wasn't avoiding danger, it was running headlong into it.

Try it yourself next time. It's easy.

That was usually enough to get them to leave her alone. They'd shrug and stumble away, dumbfounded.

Rita, who'd only just turned sixteen, didn't understand why she was so gifted in battle. She'd have been happier having a knack at baking meat pies, or knowing just where a sow wanted scratching, but apparently God had a sense of humor. He must have noticed her dozing during the sermons all those Sundays her parents had taken her to church.

Special Forces was a place for individualists, for people with authority problems. Everyone in the squad was supposedly a vicious murderer who'd been given the choice between the army and the noose. They were guys who'd as soon shoot a person as talk to him, and they didn't discriminate between friendlies and Mimics when they were letting fly with 20mm rounds. It was hard duty, and they were always looking for more warm bodies to fill the spots left by all the KIAs.

In fact, Rita's unit turned out to be a squad full of battle-hardened vets. If you melted down all the medals earned in that squad, you could have made one hell of an Olympic-class weightlifting barbell.

The squad was full of badasses who had been through Hell and back so many times they were on a first-name basis with the Devil. When shit started flying, they started telling jokes. Not the kind of jokes you told your mother over dinner, either. Contrary to their reputation, however, there were some good guys in the bunch. Rita took to her new comrades immediately.

A first lieutenant by the name of Arthur Hendricks held the squad together. He had gleaming blond hair, piercing blue eyes, and a beautiful wife so delicate you had to be careful not to break her when giving her a hug. No matter how minor the operation, Hendricks would always give his wife a call beforehand, for which he was constantly derided by the rest of the squad.

In a squad where everyone, men and women both, used language that would have sent a nun into cardiac arrest, Hendricks was the only man who never uttered a single profanity. At first he treated Rita like a little sister, much to her consternation. She'd never admit it, but she grew to like it.

Rita had been in the squad for about half a year when she became trapped in the time loop that had dictated the rhythm of her life ever since. The battle that would turn Rita Vrataski into the Valkyrie was a special operation even by U.S. Special Forces standards. The president was up for reelection, and he wanted to deliver a military victory to secure his own.

Over the objections of his generals and the media, he poured it all into the operation, every tank with treads, every attack chopper that could stay airborne, and over ten thousand platoons of Jacketed soldiers. Their goal: to regain control of the Florida peninsula. It was the most dangerous, most reckless, and by far the hardest battle Rita had ever seen.

Special Forces had a lot of four-letter words in their vocabulary, but *fear* wasn't one of them. Even so, it took more than one squad to turn around a hopeless war against a superior enemy. A Jacket granted superhuman strength, but that alone didn't turn people into superheroes. During the Second World War, Erich Hartmann had shot down 352 planes on the Russian Front, but Germany still lost the war. If the brass drafted plans that called for the impossible, the mission would fail, simple as that.

After the battle, derelict Jackets littered the Florida peninsula, their shattered shells serving as coffins for the corpses inside.

Rita Vrataski had somehow managed to toe the piano-wire-thin line that snaked between life and death. She had bent her pile driver before losing it entirely. She was low on ammo. She clutched her 20mm rifle so tightly it might as well have been welded to her hand. Fighting back the urge to vomit, she stripped batteries from the bodies of her fallen friends. She cradled her rifle in her arms.

"You look like you're having a bad day."

It was Hendricks. He sat down next to Rita where she was squatting in a hollow on the ground and looked up at the sky as though he were trying to pick shapes out of the clouds. Right in front of them, a javelin, screaming its high-pitched wail, shot into the ground. Thick black smoke billowed from the impact crater. Images of Pittsfield burning against a red sky filled Rita's thoughts.

Hendricks knew he had to walk Rita back from wherever she was. "My mother once told me that in parts of China, they mix animal blood with their tea."

Rita couldn't speak. Her throat was sandpaper, and she doubted whether she could even manage to swallow.

Hendricks went on. "The nomads there can all ride horses. Men, women, even the children. In the Middle Ages, it was their mobility that enabled them to conquer the bulk of Eurasia. Not even Europe was spared. They came from the east, moving through one country after another—savage foreigners who sipped blood from teacups—drawing nearer and nearer. It's enough to give you nightmares. Some people think it was actually those Chinese nomads who gave rise to the vampire legends of Eastern Europe."

". . . Lieutenant?"

"My little story boring you?"

"I'm all right now, Lieutenant. I'm sorry. It won't happen again."

"Hey, we all need a break sometimes. Especially in a marathon like this. Just a little more, it'll be time to hit the showers. I promise." He finished speaking and moved on to the next soldier. Rita rejoined the fray.

And then she saw it. One Mimic that stood out from the rest. It didn't look different from the others—another bloated dead frog in a sea of waterlogged amphibians. But there was something about this one that set it apart. Maybe spending so much time in such proximity to death had sharpened senses she didn't know she had, revealing secrets that lay hidden from normal sight.

When she killed that Mimic, the time loop began.

There was always one Mimic at the heart of the network, a queen of sorts. Its outward appearance was the same as the others. Just as all pigs looked alike to someone not in the business of raising pigs, the difference between that Mimic and the rest was one only Rita could see. Somehow, as she fought and slew countless Mimics, she began to tell them apart. It was something subliminal, bordering on instinct. She couldn't have explained the difference if she tried.

The easiest place to hide a tree was in the forest.

The easiest place to hide an officer was in among the grunts.

The Mimic at the heart of each pack was hiding in plain sight. Think of it as the server of the network.

When you kill the server, the Mimic network emits a specific type of signal. The scientists would later identify it as a tachyon pulse, or some other particle that could travel through time, but Rita didn't really understand any of that. The important part was that the signal emitted by Mimics that had lost their server traveled back in time to warn them of the imminent danger they faced.

The danger appeared in the memory of the Mimics as a portent, a window into the future. The Mimics that received this vision could modify their actions to safely navigate the pending danger. This was only one of many technologies discovered by that advanced race from a distant star. The process, built into the design of each crèche machine, served as a warning system to prevent some freak accident from upsetting a xenoforming plan that had taken so long to place in motion.

But the Mimics weren't the only ones who could benefit from these signals. Kill a Mimic server while in electrical contact with it, and a human would receive the same gift of foresight meant for the network. The tachyon signal sent into the past doesn't distinguish between Mimic and human, and when it came, humans perceived the portent as a hyperrealistic dream, accurate in every detail.

To truly defeat a Mimic strike force, you have to first destroy their network and all the backups it contains, then destroy the server Mimic. Otherwise, no matter how many different strategies you try, the Mimics will always develop a counterstrategy that ensures their survival.

1. Destroy the antenna.
2. Massacre every Mimic being used as backup for the network.
3. Once the possibility for transmissions to the past has been eliminated, destroy the server.

Three simple steps to escape to the future. It took Rita 211 passes through the loop to figure them out.

No one Rita told would believe her. The army was used to dealing in concrete facts. No one was interested in far-fetched stories involving time loops. When Rita finally broke out of the loop and reached the future, she learned that Arthur Hendricks had died. He was one of twenty-eight thousand killed in the battle.

In the two days Rita had spent in an endless circle of fighting, she'd managed to research the history of war, scour the feeds for information about the Mimics, and enlist a goofball engineer to make her a battle axe. She had succeeded in breaking the loop, in changing her own future, yet Hendricks's name still ended up with the letters KIA printed beside it.

Rita finally understood. This was what war really was. Every soldier who died in battle was nothing more than another figure in the calculus of estimated casualties. Their hardships, joys, and fears never entered into the equation. Some would live, others would die. It was all up to the impartial god of death called probability. With the benefit of her experience in the time loop, Rita would be able to beat the odds for some and save certain people in the future. But there would always be those she could not save. People with fathers, mothers, friends, maybe even brothers, sisters, wives, husbands, children. If she could only repeat the 211th loop, maybe she could find a way to save Hendricks—but at what cost? Rita Vrataski was alone in the time loop, and in order for her to make it out, someone would have to die.

Hendricks made one last phone call before that battle. He learned he had just become a father, and he was upset that the picture of his kid he'd printed out and taped inside his Jacket had gotten dirty. He wanted to go home, but he put the mission first. Rita had heard the phone conversation 212 times now. She knew it by heart.

Rita was awarded a medal for her distinguished service in the battle—the Order of the Valkyrie, given to soldiers who killed over one hundred Mimics in a single battle. They had created the honor just for her. And why not? The only soldier on the entire planet who could kill that many Mimics in a single battle was Rita Vrataski.

When the president pinned the gleaming medal on Rita's chest, he lauded her as an angel of vengeance on the battlefield and declared her a national treasure. She had paid for that medal with the blood of her brothers and sisters.

She didn't shed a tear. Angels don't cry.

5

Rita was redeployed. The name Full Metal Bitch and the awe it inspired rippled through the ranks. A top secret research team was created to study the time loop. After poking, prodding, and probing Rita, the lab coats drafted a report claiming it was possible that the loops had altered Rita's brain, that this was the cause of her headaches, and half a dozen other things that didn't actually answer any questions. If it meant wiping the Mimics off the face of the earth, she didn't care if their space-feeds split her skull in two.

The president had given Rita authority to act with total autonomy on the battlefield. She spoke less and less with the other members of her squad. She had a rental locker in New York where she stored the medals that kept pouring in.

6

Rita was stationed in Europe. The war went on.

7

North Africa.

When Rita heard their next assignment would be on some islands in the Far East, she was glad. Asian corpses would be a fresh change from the usual blacks and whites of the Western front. Of course, no matter how much raw fish they ate over there, the blood still came gushing out the same shade of red when a Mimic javelin ripped up a man and his Jacket. When all was said and done, she'd probably tire of seeing them, too.

8

Rita was familiar with cormorant fishing, a traditional Japanese technique. The fishermen tie a snare at the base of the trained cormorant's neck just tight enough to prevent it from swallowing any of the larger fish it catches, and then play out enough rope to enable the bird to dive into the water and fish. Once the cormorant has a fish, the fishermen pull the bird back and make it spit out its catch. Rita felt that her relationship to the army was a lot like a cormorant's relationship to a fisherman.

Rita was in the army because that was how she made her living. Her job was to go out and kill Mimics and bring their corpses back to her masters. In return, they provided her with everything she needed to live and took care of life's little annoyances without her ever having to know they were there. It was a give and take relationship, and in her mind it was fair.

Rita took no pleasure in the notion of being the savior of the earth, but if that's what the army wanted, so be it. In dark times the world needed a figure for people to rally behind.

Japan's quarantine line was on the verge of collapse. If the enemy managed to break through at Kotoiushi, Mimics would swarm the industrial complex on the main island. With the cutting-edge factories and technologies Japan brought to the table lost, there would be an estimated 30 percent drop in the effectiveness of the Jackets they used to wage the war. The ramifications would be felt throughout the UDF.

Without someone to interrupt the tachyon transmissions, the battle would never end. Technically it was possible to drive them back with an overwhelming show of force. After several loops the Mimics would realize they couldn't win, and they would withdraw with as few casualties as possible. But that wasn't the same as defeating them. They would simply retreat beneath the ocean, out of humanity's reach, and gather their strength. Once they had assembled an insurmountable force, they would attack again, and there would be no stopping them a second time.

Fighting a war with the Mimics was a lot like playing a game with a child. They had decided they were going to win before the game had even started, and they wouldn't give up until they won. Little by little, humanity was losing ground.

The duration of the Mimic time loops was approximately thirty hours. Rita repeated each loop only once. The first time through a battle she assessed the casualties her squad sustained; the second time through she won. In that first pass she could see what the strategy was and learn who died. But the lives of her friends were in the merciless hands of fate. That couldn't be changed.

Before each battle, Rita secluded herself to clear her thoughts. One of the privileges of her station was that Rita had her own private room that no one was allowed to enter.

Rita's squad understood that the thirty hours before a battle were a special time for her. The average soldier in the squad wasn't aware of the time loop, but they knew that Rita had her reasons for not wanting to talk to anyone in the time leading up to battle. They kept their distance out of respect. Even though space was exactly what Rita wanted, it still made her feel alone.

Rita was admiring the sparkling waters of the Pacific from her perch in the sky lounge. The only structure on Flower Line Base taller than Rita's tower was a nearby radio antenna. The tower was practically begging to be the first target when the Mimics came ashore. You could only laugh at the audacity of locating an officers' lounge in such a vulnerable location. This was the trouble with countries that hadn't been invaded yet.

Japan had largely managed to escape the ravages of the war. If the island had been located a little further from Asia, it would have been reduced to desert long ago. If it had been any closer, the Mimics would have invaded before moving on to the continent. The peace Japan enjoyed all came down to luck.

The area set aside for the officers' lounge was needlessly large and almost completely empty. The view it afforded of the ocean was fit for a five-star hotel. By contrast, the heavy duty pipe-frame bed that stood in the middle of the room seemed to have been chosen as a joke.

Rita pressed a button. The liquid crystal embedded in the blast-resistant glass opacified, obscuring the view. She had chosen the officers' reception room for her quarters because it was a place the other members of her squad weren't likely to visit. The operating systems embedded in the bodies of her squadmates had been programmed for war. They wouldn't set foot in a building that made for such an ostentatious target. Rita didn't care for it much herself.

To allay her fears, a Japanese tech had explained that the glass was interwoven with carbon fibers, giving it strength on par with the shell of a Jacket. If the stuff was so great, Rita wondered why it didn't seem to work that well on the front lines. At least here she was alone. The next day she might have to watch one of her friends die. She didn't want to have to look them in the eye.

A soft knock roused Rita from her thoughts. The glass at the entrance to the lounge was also embedded with liquid crystal. It was set to opaque with the rest.

"I don't appreciate distractions within minus thirty hours. Just leave me alone."

There was no reply. She sensed an odd presence from the other side of the door. It felt like a small animal being hunted by a pack of wolves, or a woman being stalked down a dark alley. It could only be Shasta.

Rita pressed the button. The glass cleared to reveal the petite Native American woman standing at the door. First Lieutenant Shasta Raylle was older than Rita and, technically, outranked her, but the Valkyrie didn't have to bend over backward for any engineer. Still, Rita found Shasta's deference and politesse endearing.

Thud.

Shasta bumped her forehead against the glass. She'd mistaken the suddenly transparent glass for an open doorway and walked right into it. She was holding something in the hand she pressed to her head. She crouched on the ground, trembling like a leaf. It was hard to believe the brain in that head could be so brilliant. Then again, maybe that's how geniuses were. Some people called Rita a military genius, and she wasn't all that different from everyone else. The only thing about her that was especially unique was her ability to focus. Shasta's thoughts were probably consumed by whatever it was she held in her hand, just as Rita's were by the coming battle.

Rita opened the door halfway. Shasta's glasses were still askew from the impact with the glass. She adjusted them as she stood.

"I'm sorry to bother you. But there was something I just had to show you. I'm really, really sorry." Shasta lowered her head and bumped it against the door that still blocked half of the entryway. This time she hit the corner.

Thud.

"Ow." Shasta squatted on the ground again.

"No need to apologize. You're always welcome, Lieutenant. Without you, who would look after my Jacket?"

Shasta sprang to her feet, eyes moist with tears.

"You called me lieutenant again! Call me Shasta, please."

"But, Lieutenant—"

"Shasta! I just want everyone to talk to me like a normal person."

"All right, all right. Shasta."

"That's better."

Rita smiled. "So . . . what was it you wanted to show me?"

"Right," Shasta said. "Look at this. You won't believe it."

Shasta opened her hand. Rita looked intently at the strange object resting in her tiny palm. Only slightly larger than a 9mm bullet, it was intricately shaped and painted bright red. Rita had heard of people who painted the tips of their bullets a separate color to distinguish between types of ammunition, but never the entire casing.

She picked it up. It was shaped like a person.

Shasta raced on. "This is supposed to be secret, right? Someone on the base told me about them. I went all the way to Tateyama to get it. It took almost all the money I had on me to win it."

"Win it?"

"You put money in the machine, turn the knob, and one of these figures pops out in a little plastic bubble."

"Is it some kind of toy?"

"Oh no, it's a valuable collector's item. The rare ones can trade for over a hundred dollars each."

"A hundred dollars for *this*?"

"That's right." Shasta nodded gravely.

Rita held the tiny figure up to the white lights of the room. Upon closer examination, it was clearly meant to resemble a soldier wearing a Jacket. That it was painted red and wielding a battle axe could only mean it was supposed to be Rita's Jacket. "They did a good job. Even the fins look just like the real ones. I guess military secrets aren't what they used to be."

"They use professional modelers. All they need is a glimpse to make something almost exactly like the original. The models made in Japan are the best. They can auction for a lot of money."

"What a waste of perfectly good talent." Rita flipped the figure over in her hand. Etched across the feet were the words MADE IN CHINA. "China still has time to make toys? I heard they can't even keep up with the production of the Jacket control chips."

"They've got a bigger workforce to go around. Remember that senator who was forced to resign after he said China could afford to lose as many people as there are in the entire United States and still have over a billion left? Well, they actually have lost millions of people down in the south, but they've been able to throw enough resources at it to hold the line."

"It's hard to believe we come from the same planet."

"America's at war, and we still find the time to turn out terrible movies."

Rita couldn't argue with that.

The UDF existed to protect a world obsessed with creating worthless piles of crap, Rita thought. It was amazing how people could pour their hearts and souls into such trivial things. Not that this was necessarily a bad thing. No one appreciated that more than Rita, whose only skill was killing.

"I have lots more." Shasta pulled a handful of figures from her overalls.

"What's this? Some sort of pig-frog from the dark reaches of the Amazon?"

"That's a Mimic."

"So much for your professional modelers."

"This is what they look like in the movies. So it is the real thing as far as the public's concerned, anyway. Believe me, this is what's in the movies, down to the last wrinkle."

"What about this one?"

"You should know. It's Rita Vrataski—you!"

The figure was lean, prodigiously endowed, and sported curly blonde hair. It was hard to find a single feature that even remotely resembled Rita. As it happened, Rita had actually met the actress cast to play her in the movies once. It was difficult to say she didn't fit the role of a Jacket jockey, since Rita herself hardly did. But the woman they picked for the part was far too glamorous for a soldier fighting on the front lines.

Rita compared her figure with that of the Mimic. Suddenly, the Mimic modeler wasn't looking so far off.

"Mind if I hold on to this?" Rita picked up the Full Metal Bitch figurine that bore her no resemblance.

"What?"

"You won't miss one, will you?"

Shasta's reaction was somewhere between that of a sleeping cat kicked out of its favorite spot in bed and a five-year-old whose aunt had denied her the last piece of chocolate macadamia nut toffee because she'd been saving it for herself. The look on her face would have sent applications to MIT plummeting if prospective students had known she was an alumna who had graduated at the top of her class.

Rita reconsidered her request. People like Shasta who went to hyper-competitive upper-crust universities were probably more likely than most to randomly explode if pushed. "Sorry, bad joke. I shouldn't tease you like that."

"No, I'm the one who should apologize," Shasta said. "It's just that it's kind of, well, really rare. I mean, I bought every single bubble in the machine, and that was the only one that came out."

"Don't worry. I wouldn't dream of taking it from you."

"Thanks for understanding. I'm really sorry. Here, why don't you take this one instead? It's supposed to be pretty rare too."

"What is it?"

"It's the engineer assigned to Rita's squad in the movie. So it's basically . . . me." A nervous laugh escaped Shasta's lips.

It was the worst cliché of a female engineer Rita had ever seen. Rail thin, freckled, exaggerated facial features at the extreme edge of the probability curve. If there were ever a ten-millimeter-high perfectionist who would never misplace so much as a single screw or run the risk of kissing a member of the opposite sex, this was it. Of course the real, brilliant engineer it was supposedly based on probably hit her head on her own locker at least twice a day, so it just went to show that you never knew.

Shasta looked up at Rita with worry in her eyes. "Don't you like it?"

"It doesn't look anything like you."

"Neither does yours."

They looked at each other.

"All right, thanks. I'll keep it. For luck."

Shasta lifted another figure when Ralph Murdoch, the requisite camera hanging from his thick neck, walked in.

"Good morning, ladies."

Rita cocked one rust-red eyebrow at the arrival of her unwelcome guest. Her face hardened to steel. The sudden change in Rita's demeanor startled Shasta, who looked as though she couldn't decide whether she wanted to hide from Rita behind this strange hulk of a journalist or the other way around. After a few awkward moments of hesitation, she opted for taking cover behind Rita.

"How did you get in here?" Rita made no attempt to hide her disdain.

"I'm a registered member of your personal staff. Who would stop me?"

"You're your own staff, and we both know it. You can leave now." Rita didn't care much for this man and his never-saw-a-speck-of-battlefield-mud running shoes. People like him and Shasta could meet and talk in total safety whenever the mood took them. His words were never limned with the dread of knowing you would have to watch your friends die in the next battle. It was that dread, that certainty, that kept Rita away from her squadmates, the only family she had left. Nothing this rambling fool would ever have to deal with in his entire life.

"That'd be a shame after coming all the way up here," Murdoch said. "I happened upon an interesting piece of news, and I thought I'd share it with you."

"Send it to the *New York Times*. I'll be happy to read all about it."

"Trust me, you'll wanna hear this."

"I'm not all that interested in what you find interesting."

"The Japanese troops are going to have some PT. Punishment for troublemaking last night."

"I asked you to leave. I'm never in a good mood before battle."

"Don't you want to come watch? They're going to do some sort of samurai-style training. I'd love to hear the Valkyrie's take on the whole affair."

"Your mother must have been disappointed when the abortion only killed your conscience," Rita said.

"Such talk from a nice, sweet girl like you."

"I'd say it next time too, but I can't be bothered."

"Come again?"

"Believe me, I'd rather not."

Murdoch raised an eyebrow. "Okay, so you talk trash and nonsense. Two for one."

"I guess it must be catching."

"Fine, so I have no conscience and I'm going straight to Hell. You told me the same thing in Indonesia when I took those pictures of the crying kid running from a pack of Mimics."

"Hell's too good for you. You'd just find a way to get a picture of Satan and use it to worm your way through Heaven's back door."

"I'll take that as a compliment."

A smile spread across the Valkyrie's lips. It was the same smile that came to her in those dark hours on the battlefield, when it was at least hidden behind her helmet. Shasta's body tensed. Murdoch took a step back without even realizing it.

"Well," the Full Metal Bitch said, "I'm about to step into Hell. And until I do, I don't want to see your face again."

9

Rita ended up going to watch the PT. Shasta didn't. The only person near Rita was that damned Murdoch. The rest of her squad maintained a respectful distance.

That was when Rita's eyes met that challenge from the field, that gaze bearing the weight of the world. There was something about the kid that Rita liked. She started walking toward him.

She strode with purpose, each step a perfect movement designed to propel a Jacket across a battlefield with total efficiency. She advanced across the field effortlessly and without a sound. To get 100 percent out of a Jacket, a soldier had to be able to walk across a room full of eggs without cracking a single one. That meant being able to perfectly distribute their body weight with every step.

The soldier was still staring at Rita. She walked right to him, then made a ninety-degree turn and headed toward the tent where the brigadier general was sitting. She gave him one regulation salute.

The brigadier general cast a doubtful glance at Rita. Rita was a sergeant major by rank, but she was also in the U.S. corps, so their actual relative places in military hierarchy were a little muddy.

Rita remembered this man. He had been attached at the hip to the general who had made a beeline to shake Rita's hand at the start of the frivolous reception held to welcome the Special Forces. There were plenty of officers who had climbed the ranks without ever fighting on the front lines, but this one seemed to have a special love for grandstanding and ass-kissing.

They spoke briefly, the general seemingly bemused and Rita's stance and body language well-practiced. Then Rita returned to the field, walking past the ranks of men who seemed to bow before her. She chose a spot beside the soldier who'd been staring daggers at her and started her iso push-up. She could feel the heat of his body radiating through the chill air between them.

The soldier didn't move. Rita didn't move. The sun hung high in the sky, slowly roasting their skin. Rita spoke in a low voice only the soldier beside her could hear:

"Do I have something on my face?"

"Not that I can see."

Other than a slightly odd intonation, the soldier's Burst was clear and easy to understand. Nothing like back in North Africa. People from the former French colonies couldn't speak Burst to save their lives.

Burst English, or simply Burst, was a language created to deal with the problem of communication in an army comprised of soldiers from dozens of countries. It had a pared-down vocabulary and as few grammatical irregularities as possible. When they drafted the language, they deliberately struck all the profanities from the official vocabulary list, but you couldn't keep a bunch of soldiers from adding "fuck" in its various noun, verb, and adjective forms to everything anyway.

"You've been staring at me for a while now."

"I guess I have," he said.

"There something you want from me?"

"Nothing I want to discuss like this."

"Then let's wait until this is done."

"Shit-for-brains Kiriya! You're slipping!" the lieutenant barked. Rita, with the disinterested expression of someone who'd never had a need for human contact her entire life, continued her iso push-up.

Iso push-ups were a lot rougher than they looked. Beads of sweat formed along your hairline, streamed past your temples, ran into your eyes—making them burn from the salt—and traced the line of your neck before falling from your chest. Having to endure that itch as it makes its way down your body was a lot like what a soldier had to endure encased in a Jacket. *This samurai training isn't completely worthless after all*, Rita decided.

When things got too hard to bear, it was best to let your mind wander. Rita let her thoughts drift from her own body's screams of protest to the surroundings. The brigadier general from the General Staff Office looked baffled by the intruder in his proceedings. For him, a man who had never experienced a moment of real armed conflict, maybe this training field, with its gentle ocean breezes, was part of the war. To people who had never breathed in that mixture of blood, dust, and burning metal that pervaded a battlefield, it was easy to imagine that deployment was war, that training was war, that climbing some career ladder was war. There was only one person for whom the war extended to that tranquil day before the battle: a woman named Rita Vrataski and her time loops.

Rita had often dreamt that someday she would come across another person who experienced the loops. She'd even come up with a phrase they could use to identify themselves to each other. A phrase only Rita knew. A phrase the two of them would share.

For another person to be caught in a time loop, it would mean that someone other than Rita had destroyed a Mimic server by accident. Just as Rita was forced to leave people outside the time loop behind, this person would have no choice but to leave her behind. He would be alone.

She might not be able to travel through the time loop with him—though she also might be able to, and the thought terrified her—but she could give him advice either way. Share his solitude. Tell him how to break out of the loop, knowledge it had taken Rita 211 deaths to learn. He would fight through his doubts, the way Rita had. He would become a great warrior.

Deep in a quiet corner of Rita's heart, she was sure no one would ever come to tell her the words only she knew.

The Mimic tachyon signal was the pinnacle of an alien technology, a technology that had enabled them to conquer the vastness of space. Rita's entrapment in the time loop during the battle to recapture Florida had been an impossible stroke of luck for humanity. If not for that chance occurrence, the earth would have fallen to xenoforming. Not just humans, but virtually every species on the planet, would already be extinct.

Rita's fame grew with each battle, and her loneliness with it. She had broken out of the time loop, but she felt as though she were still reliving the same day. Her one hope was that humanity's victory, the day when every last Mimic had been blasted to extinction, would somehow rid her of her terrible isolation. Until then, she would continue to play her unique role in the conflict.

Rita didn't mind the battles. She didn't have to think to fight. When she climbed into her red Jacket, the sadness, the laughter, the memory that haunted her more than the rest—it all slipped away. The battlefield, swirling with smoke and gunpowder, was Rita's home.

PT ended less than an hour later. The general, the bile in his mouth forgotten, hurried off to the barracks.

As Rita stood, the man beside her staggered to his feet. He wasn't particularly tall for a Jacket jockey. He was young, but he wore his fatigues as though he'd been born in them. His clothes looked as though they'd just come from the factory, so there was something strangely jarring about his appearance. His lips were twisted in a Mona Lisa smile that did a good job of concealing his age.

The number 157 was scrawled in Arabic numerals on the back of his hand. Rita didn't know what it meant, but it was an odd thing to do. Odd enough that Rita didn't think she'd be forgetting him anytime soon. She had heard of soldiers taping their blood type to the soles of their feet in the days before Jackets were standard-issue, but she'd never heard of a soldier who kept notes in ballpoint pen on the back of his hand.

"So you wanted to talk. What is it?"

"Ah, right," he said.

"Well? Get on with it, soldier. I'm a patient girl, but there's a battle tomorrow, and I have things to do."

"I, uh, have an answer to your question." He hesitated like a high school drama student reading from a bad script. "Japanese restaurants don't charge for green tea."

Rita Vrataski, the savior of humanity, the Valkyrie, the nineteen-year-old girl, let her mask slip.

The Full Metal Bitch began to cry.

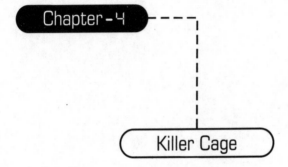

Chapter - 4

Killer Cage

I

"Shit, it's started! Don't get your balls blown off, gents!"

Battle 159.

I dart forward, my Jacket's Doppler set to max.

I spot a target, fire, duck. A javelin whizzes past my head.

"Who's up there? You're too far forward! You wanna get yourself killed?"

The lieutenant said the same thing every time. I wiped sand from my helmet. Thunder erupted from the shells crisscrossing the sky. I glanced at Ferrell and nodded.

This time the battle would end. If I stood by and watched as Yonabaru and Ferrell died, they wouldn't be coming back. It all came down to this. There was no repeating this battle. The fear that clawed at my guts wasn't fear of death, it was fear of the unknown. I wanted to throw down my rifle and axe and find a bed to hide under.

A normal reaction—the world wasn't meant to repeat itself. I grinned in spite of the butterflies in my stomach. I was struggling with the same fear everyone struggles with. I was putting my life— the only one I had—on the line.

"You're not actually caught in a time loop," Rita had explained to me. My experiences of the 158 previous battles were real; it was me who didn't really exist. Whoever it was that had been there for the excruciating pain, hopelessness, and the hot piss in his Jacket, he was only a shattered memory now.

Rita told me that from the point of view of the person with the memory, there was no difference between having had an actual experience and only having the memory of it. Sounded like philosophical bullshit to me. Rita didn't seem to understand it all that well either.

I remember reading a comic, back when I still read comics, about a guy who used a time machine to change the past. It seemed to me that if the past changed, then the guy from the future who went back in time to change it should have disappeared—like the guy in those old *Back to the Future* movies—but the comic glossed over those details.

I had become an unwilling voyeur to the dreams of the Mimics. In my very first battle, the one where Rita saved my life, I had unknowingly killed one of those Mimics she called "servers." In every battle since then, from the second right up to the 158th, Rita had killed the server. But the network between me and the server had already been established the instant I killed it, meaning I was the one trapped in the loop, and that Rita had been freed.

The Mimics used the loop to alter the future to their advantage. The javelin that missed Yonabaru in the second battle had been meant for me. My chance encounter with a Mimic when I ran from the base hadn't had anything to do with chance. They'd been hunting me all along. If it hadn't been for Rita, they would have had me for breakfast, lunch, and dinner.

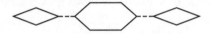

The fighting continued. Chaos stalked the battlefield.

I slid into a crater with the rest of my squad to avoid getting ventilated by a sniper javelin shot. The squad had moved a hundred meters nearer to the coast since the start of battle. The conical hole we had taken cover in was courtesy of the previous night's GPS-guided bombardment. A stray round landed near my feet, spraying sand into the air.

"Just like Okinawa," remarked Ferrell, his back pressed against the wall of earth.

Yonabaru squeezed off another round. "Musta been a helluva fight."

"We were surrounded, just like now. Ran out of ammo and things got ugly."

"You're gonna jinx us."

"I don't know—" Ferrell sprang up from the cover of the crater, fired his rifle, then sank back against the wall. "I got it in my head that this battle's going somewhere. Just a feeling."

"Shit, Sarge is talkin' happy talk. Better watch out we don't get struck by lightning."

"You have any doubts, just watch our newest recruit in action," Ferrell said. "Wouldn't surprise me to see him get up and dance the jitterbug just to piss the Mimics off."

"I don't know the jitterbug," I said.

"No shit."

"Maybe I'll give that pretty battle axe of yours a try." Yonabaru nodded at the gleaming slab of tungsten carbide in my Jacket's grip.

"You'd just hurt yourself."

"That's discrimination is what that is."

Same old, same old. Everyone talking over each other, no one listening.

"Bogies at two o'clock!"

"Our thirty-fifth customer of the day!"

"Which one of you assholes just sent me this huge-ass file? We're in the middle of a fuckin' war, if you haven't been keepin' up!"

"Man, I need some smokes."

"Shut the fuck up and shoot!"

The front line edged out of cover and leveled their rifles at the approaching throng. Bullets pierced the air, but the Mimic blitz kept coming. I gripped the handle of my axe.

Without warning, a bomb fell from the sky. The laser-guided precision munition smashed the bedrock, digging deep into the earth before detonating. The Mimics tumbled into the crater.

A crimson Jacket appeared amid the downpour of earth and clay. Tungsten carbide slashed away at flailing limbs and those thick, froggy torsos. After a few minutes, nothing was left moving. Nothing alien anyway.

Static filled my ears, then her voice came through. "Sorry to keep you waiting." The Full Metal Bitch stood, hefting an enormous battle axe, amid our sand-colored platoon. Her gunmetal red armor glistened in the sun.

I lifted my hand so she could pick me out of the crowd. "We just got here ourselves."

"What's the Full Metal Bitch doin' here?" Yonabaru forgot all about taking cover and stared stupidly at her Jacket. I would have paid good money for a look at his face.

Rita addressed Ferrell. "I need to talk to whoever's in charge of this platoon. Patch me in."

Ferrell opened a channel between Rita and the lieutenant. "You're good to go."

"This is Rita Vrataski. I have a request for the officer in charge of the 3rd Platoon of the 17th Company, 3rd Battalion, 12th Regiment, 301st Armored Infantry Division. I need to borrow Keiji Kiriya. That all right with you?"

She didn't state her rank or division. In a military culture where the sky was whatever color your ranking officer said it was, only the Valkyrie was free to operate outside the chain of command. Even back in that first battle, it hadn't been the Full Metal Bitch who cradled my head as I lay dying. It was Rita Vrataski.

The lieutenant's reply was unsure. "Kiriya? Maybe you'd like someone with more experience, someone—"

"Yes or no?"

"Well, uh, yes."

"I appreciate your help. Sarge, how 'bout you? Mind if I borrow Kiriya?"

Ferrell shrugged his approval, his Jacketed shoulders rising like an ocean wave.

"Thank you, Sarge."

"See that he doesn't do any jitterbugging near our squad."

"Jitterbugging? That some sort of code?" Rita asked.

"Just a figure of speech."

"Keiji, what's all this about?"

"Sorry, Sarge. I'll explain later," I said.

"We'll hit 'em from twelve o'clock."

"Uh, right."

"Hey, Keiji! If you see a vending machine, pick me up some smokes!" Yonabaru called out right before I disconnected from the comm link.

Rita chuckled at Yonabaru's wisecrack. "You've got a good squad. You ready?"

"Be gentle."

"I'm always gentle."

"That's not the way I hear it."

"Just worry about the Mimics, okay?"

Slamming against the sides of the impact crater, scrabbling, and finally climbing over one another, Mimics had begun to push out from the hole Rita had blasted in the ground. We dove into the pack headfirst. It was wall-to-wall bloated frogs.

Run. Fire. Retreat. Fresh magazine. Run some more. Fire. Breathe.

Precision bombs hunted for the Mimics where they hid. Smoke spiraled skyward where they had found their quarry. Sand and dirt followed the smoke into the air, and chunks of Mimic flesh weren't far behind. We rushed into the crater and took out everything the bombs left. Root 'em out, mow 'em down.

Even when you were just repeating the same day over and over, life on the battlefield was anything but routine. If the angle of your swing was off by so much as a degree, it could set off a chain of events that would change the entire outcome of the battle. A Mimic you let slip through one minute would be mowing through your friends the next. With each soldier that died, the line grew weaker, until it eventually collapsed under the strain. All because your axe swung at forty-seven degrees instead of forty-eight.

There were more Mimics than I could count. Dots filled the Doppler screen. The rule of thumb was that it took a squad of ten

Jackets to bring down one Mimic. Even then, to make it an even match the squad had to be fanned out to spray the damn thing with bullets until there weren't any bullets left.

Rita was in constant motion. She swung her axe with the ease of a child swinging a plastic toy sword. The air was thick with Mimic parts. Another step, another swing, another limb. Wash, rinse, repeat.

I'd never seen anything like it. Javelins carried death through the air. I was close enough to reach out and touch half a dozen Mimics. In spite of the danger all around me, I felt an uncanny calm. I had someone to watch my back. Rita was a filter that distilled and neutralized the fear. I was in the valley of the shadow of death, no two fucking ways about it, but I had Rita at my side.

I learned to survive by mimicking Rita's skill with the axe, and in the process, I'd come to know her every move—which foot she'd take the next step with, which Mimic she'd strike first when surrounded. I knew when she would swing her axe, and when she would run. All that and more was hardcoded into my operating system.

Rita sidestepped danger and moved through the enemy ranks, carving a path of perfectly executed destruction. The only things she left standing were targets she couldn't be bothered to kill. I was only too happy to mop up after her. We'd never trained together, but we moved like twins, veterans of countless battles at each other's side.

Four Mimics came for Rita at once—bad odds, even for the Valkyrie. She was still off balance from her last swing. With my free hand, I gave her a gentle nudge. For a split second she was startled, but it didn't take her long to understand what I'd done.

She really was a master. In less than five minutes, she'd learned to work in tandem with me. When she realized I could use a free arm or leg to knock her clear of an attack, she turned and faced the next enemy head on, without any intent of dodging. A Mimic foreleg came within a hand's breadth of her face and she didn't even flinch.

We worked as a single unit. We tore through the enemy with frightening power, always keeping the other's Jacket in the corner of our eyes. We didn't need words or gestures. Every motion, every footstep said all that needed to be said.

Our enemy may have evolved the ability to rewind time, but humanity had evolved a few tricks of its own. There were people who could keep a Jacket in tip-top condition, people who could conjure up strategies and handle logistics, people who could provide support on the front lines, and last but not least, people who were natural-born killers. People could adapt themselves to their environment and their experiences in any number of ways. An enemy that could look into the future and perceive danger fell victim to its own evolutionary atrophy. We learned faster than they could.

I had passed through death 158 times to emerge at heights no creature on this planet could aspire to in a single lifetime. Rita Vrataski had ascended even higher. We strode ahead, far from the rest of the force, an army unto ourselves. Our Jackets traced graceful clockwise spirals as we pressed on—a habit I'd picked up from Rita. Twitching mounds of carrion were all we left in our wake.

Forty-two minutes into the battle, we found it. The Mimic at the root of the whole motherfucking loop. The thread that bound us. If not for this server, I would never have drowned in my own blood, watched my guts spill onto the ground dozens of times over, wandered aimlessly through this Hell with no way out. If it weren't for this server, I would never have met Rita Vrataski.

"This is it, Keiji. You have to be the one to bring it down."

"With pleasure."

"Remember: antenna first, then the backups, then the server."

"And then we go home?"

"Not quite. When the loop ends, the real battle begins. It's not over until there isn't a Mimic left moving."

"Nothing's ever easy."

Genocide was the only way to win this war. You couldn't shave their forces down by 30 percent and claim victory. You had to destroy every last one of them. Take down the server, and the war would go on. All Rita and I could do was free our troops from the quagmire of the Mimics' time loops. A lasting victory would require more force than two soldiers alone could ever bring to bear. But on the day we did win, I could die, Rita could die, Yonabaru, Ferrell, and the rest of our platoon could die, even those cunt-lipped assholes in the 4th could die, and time would never repeat again. A new day would dawn on Earth.

Rita said taking out a Mimic server was as easy as opening a tin can. All you needed was the right opener. Catch was, up until then she'd been the only person on the planet who had one.

People of Earth, rejoice! Keiji Kiriya just found another can opener! Act now, and for every Rita Vrataski–brand can opener you purchase, you'll receive a second Keiji Kiriya–brand can opener at NO ADDITIONAL CHARGE!

Of course, you couldn't buy us separately if you wanted to. I suppose Rita and I wouldn't have made very honest sales-men. What this nightmarish time loop from the bowels of Hell hath joined together, let no man put asunder. Only Rita and I understood each other's solitude, and we would stand side by side, dicing Mimics into bite-size chunks until the bitter end.

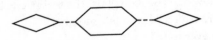

"Antenna down!"
"On to the backups."
"Copy that."
I raised my battle axe and brought it down in a swift, clean stroke—

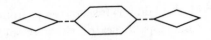

I opened my eyes. I was in bed.
I took a pen and wrote "160" on the back of my hand. Then I kicked the wall as hard as I could.

2

It's not easy telling a person something you know is going to make them cry, let alone doing it with an audience. And if Jin Yonabaru is in that audience, you're up shit creek in a concrete canoe with a hole in the bottom.

Last time it had come out sounding too forced. I was trying to think of a better way to say it, but I couldn't come up with anything short and sweet that would let Rita know that I was also experiencing the time loops. Maybe I should just tell her that. Hell, I didn't have any better ideas.

I'd never been particularly smart, and what little brains I did have were preoccupied with trying to figure out why I hadn't broken out of the loop according to plan. I'd done everything just as Rita told me, but here I was on my 160th day before the battle.

The sky over the No. 1 Training Field was as clear the 160th time as it had been the first. The ten o'clock sun beat down on us without pity. PT had just ended, and the shadows pooled at our feet were speckled with darker spots of sweat.

I was a total stranger to this woman with rust-colored hair and skin far too pale for a soldier. Her rich brown eyes fixed on me.

"So you wanted to talk. What is it?"

I was out of time, and I was fresh out of bright ideas. I'd have been better off taking her aside before PT. Too late now.

I looked at Rita and said the same bit about green tea I had before. *Hey, that didn't go so bad this time,* I thought. *Maybe she's not going to—oh, fuck.*

Tears streamed down Rita's cheeks and dripped from the point of her chin, then splashed as they landed in the palm of the hand I held out to catch them. I was still hot from exercising, but the tears burned like 20mm slugs. My heart was pounding. I was a junior high school student asking a girl to the dance. Not even battle pumped my blood pressure this much.

Rita clutched the bottom of my shirt, squeezing so tight the tips of her fingers were white. On the battlefield I could see every move coming before she made it, but here I was clueless. I'd programmed myself to dodge a thousand Mimic attacks with ease, but what good was my OS when I really needed it? My mind wandered, looking for an out. I wondered if my shirt was sweaty where she was grabbing it.

The last time, I had stood like a park statue until Rita regained her composure and spoke. Maybe after ten more trips through the loop this would all be routine. I'd know just what to say to soothe her as I held her gently against my shoulder. But that would mean reducing my interactions with the one and only person in the world who understood me to a rote performance. Something told me it was better to just stand there and take it.

Yonabaru was gaping at us like a tourist in a zoo gapes at a bear who has suddenly stood up and begun to waltz. At least I'd finally found a situation that would shut him up. Ferrell politely averted his eyes, but only halfway. And that was more or less how the rest of the platoon behaved. Fuck me. I was the dancing bear. *Don't stare. Don't say anything. Just throw your money in the can and move along.*

What was it you were supposed to do when you were nervous— picture everyone naked? No, that was for speaking in public. In training they taught us to hold ourselves together by thinking of something we enjoyed. Something that made you happy. In battle, this would probably be one of those happy things to think back on, so why was it so nerve-racking now? If God had an answer, He wasn't talking.

I took Rita by the wrist. She looked lost.

"I'm Keiji Kiriya."

"Rita. Rita Vrataski."

"I guess I should start with 'Nice to meet you.'"

"Why are you smiling?"

"I dunno. Just happy, I guess," I said.

"You're an odd one." Rita's face softened.

"Let's make a break for it." My eyes glanced over her shoulder. "My two o'clock. You ready?"

Rita and I sprinted away, leaving the men on the field scratching their heads. We slipped past the chain link fence bordering the training grounds. The breeze blowing off the sea was cool against our skin. For a while we ran for running's sake. The coastline lay far off to our left, cobalt-blue waters spreading beyond the meaningless barricade of barbed wire that lined the beach. The ocean still blue because we had fought to keep it that way. A patrol boat cutting a course parallel to our own trailed a white wake along the sharp line that divided sea and sky.

The deep shouts of the soldiers faded. The only sounds were the roar of the sea, the faraway shuffling noises of military boots on concrete, my too-loud pounding heart, and the sigh of Rita's breath.

I came to an abrupt halt and stood dumbly, just as I had before we started running. Rita couldn't cut her speed in time and came crashing into me. Another OS slip-up. I took a few awkward steps. Rita stumbled as she regained her balance. We held on to each other to keep from falling. My arm was wrapped around Rita's body and hers around mine.

The impact risked breaking any number of regulations. Her toned flesh pressed against me like reactive armor. A pleasant scent assaulted my senses. Without my Jacket, I was defenseless against any stray chemicals that chanced into the air.

"Uh, excuse me." Rita was the first to apologize.

"No, my bad. I shouldn't have stopped."

"No. I mean, excuse me, but—" she said.

"You don't have to apologize."

"I'm not trying to apologize. It's just—would you mind letting go of my hand?"

"Ah—" A red ring stood out on Rita's wrist where my fingers had gripped her skin. "Sorry."

To me, Rita was an old friend, a companion of many battles. But to her, Keiji Kiriya was a stranger she'd just met. Nothing more than an ashen silhouette from another time. Only I remembered the relief we'd felt when we stood with our backs pressed against each other. Only I had experienced the electricity that flowed between us when our eyes met in implicit understanding. Only I felt a sense of longing and devotion.

Before I joined the army, I saw a show about a man in love with a woman who'd lost her memory in an accident. He must have gone through something like what I was going through now. Hopelessly watching all the things you love in the world being carried away on the wind while you stand by powerless to prevent it.

"I'm—well . . ." I didn't even know what to say to her this time, despite the previous loop.

"This your clever way of getting the two of us out of there?"

"Yeah. I guess."

"Good. Now where exactly are we?" Rita spun on her heel as she took in her surroundings.

We stood in a wide space bordered on one side by the barbed-wire barricade and a chain-link fence on the other three. Weeds sent shoots of green through the cracks in the concrete that covered the roughly ten-thousand-square-meter enclosure.

"The No. 3 Training Field."

I'd managed to take us from one training field to another. Smooth. I'd been spending too much time with Ferrell. His love of training bordered on serious mental illness, and it had started to rub off on me.

Rita turned back to me. "It's kind of bleak."

"Sorry."

"No, I like the emptiness of it."

"You have unusual tastes."

"Is that even a taste? The place I grew up was hopelessly empty. We didn't have any oceans, though. The sky out here is—it's so brilliant," she said, her head tilted back.

"You like it? The sky?"

"Not the sky so much as the color of it. That shimmering blue."

"Then why's your Jacket red?"

A few moments of silence passed between us before she spoke again.

"The sky in Pittsfield is so washed out. Like the color of water after you've rinsed out a paintbrush with blue paint in it. Like all the water in the ground rushed up in the sky and thinned it." I gazed at Rita. She looked back at me, rich brown eyes staring into mine. "Sorry. Forget I said that," she said.

"How come?"

"It wasn't a very Rita Vrataski thing to say."

"I don't know about that."

"I do."

"Well, I thought it was nice," I said.

Rita opened her eyes wide. For an instant, they flashed with a glint of the Full Metal Bitch. The rest of her face remained still. "What'd you say?"

"I said it sounded nice."

She looked surprised at that. A lock of rust-colored hair fell to her forehead, and she raised her hand to play with it. I caught a glimpse of her eyes from between her fingers. They were filled with a strange light. She looked like a girl whose heart strings had begun to unravel, a child whose lies had been laid bare by the piercing gaze of her mother.

I broke the awkward silence. "Is something wrong?"

"No."

"I wasn't making fun of you. It's just something I wanted to say. Guess I didn't get the timing right."

"We've had a conversation like this before in an earlier loop, haven't we? But only you remember," Rita said.

"Yeah. I'm sorry."

"No, it doesn't bother me," she said, shaking her head.

"Then what's wrong?"

"Tell me what you're planning."

"Well, there's a lot I still don't understand," I said. "I need you to explain how to end the loop, for starters."

"I'm asking what you're planning to do next so I don't have to think about it."

"Are you kidding?" I asked.

"I'm dead serious."

"But you're Rita Vrataski. You always know what to do."

"It will be fun being the one outside the loop for a change."

"Not much fun for me," I said. I wondered what she meant by saying "will"; I thought she'd been freed from the loop already, after 211 times through thirty hours in Florida. I opened my mouth to ask, but she interrupted.

"I think I've earned the right to sit back and watch," she said. "I've had to handle enough shit as it is. It's your turn. The sooner you accept that, the better."

I sighed. "I know."

"Hey, don't blame me."

"Well then, it's still a little early, but my next stop is the cafeteria. I hope you're in the mood for Japanese food."

The cafeteria was noisy. In one corner, a group of soldiers was seeing who could do the most push-ups in three minutes. Another group we walked past was playing gastronomic chicken with a mystery liquid that looked like a combination of ketchup, mustard, and orange juice. At the far end of the room some guy was singing a folk song—or maybe it was an old anime theme song—that had been popular at least seventy years ago, complete with banjo accompaniment. One of the feed religions had originally used it as an anti-war song, but that wasn't the sort of detail that bothered guys who signed up with the UDF. The tune was easy to remember, and that's all it took to be a hit with a crowd of Jacket jockeys.

Let's all join the ar-my!
Let's all join the ar-my!
Let's all join the ar-my!
And kill ourselves some things!

I'd watched all this 159 times. But since I'd been caught in the loop, I hardly noticed a thing about the world outside my own head that didn't directly pertain to my way out of here. I sat quietly in a small, gray cafeteria, devoid of sound, methodically shoveling tasteless food into my mouth.

Even if tomorrow's battle went well, some of the soldiers here wouldn't be coming back. If it went poorly, even fewer would return. Everybody knew it. The Armored Infantry was Santa Claus, and battle was our Christmas. What else for the elves to do on Christmas Eve but let their hair down and drink a little eggnog.

Rita Vrataski was sitting across from me, eating the same lunch for the 160th time. She examined her 160th *umeboshi*.

"What is this?"

"*Umeboshi*. It's ume—people call it a plum, but it's more like an apricot—dried in the sun, and then pickled. You eat it."

"What's it taste like?"

"Food is like war. You have to experience it for yourself."

She poked at it two or three times with her chopsticks, then threw caution to the wind and put the whole thing in her mouth. The sourness hit her like a body blow from a heavyweight fighter and she doubled over, grabbing at her throat and chest. I could see the muscles twitching in her back.

"Like it?"

Rita worked her mouth without looking up. Her neck tensed. Something went flying out of her mouth—a perfectly clean pit skidded to a halt on her tray. She wiped the edges of her mouth as she gasped for breath.

"Not sour at all."

"Not at this cafeteria," I said. "Too many people from overseas. Go to a local place if you want the real stuff."

I picked up the *umeboshi* from my tray and popped it into my mouth. I made a show of savoring the flavor. Truth be known, it was sour enough to twist my mouth as tight as a crab's ass at low tide, but I wasn't about to give her the satisfaction of seeing that.

"Pretty good." I smacked my lips.

Rita stood, her mouth a stern line. She left me sitting at the table as she strode down the corridor between the tables, past throngs of soldiers, and up to the serving counter. There, Rachel spoke to a gorilla of a man who could reach up and touch the ceiling without so much as stretching—the same gorilla from the 4th whose fist my jaw had encountered all those loops ago. Beauty and the Beast were understandably surprised to see the subject of their conversation walk up to them. The entire cafeteria could sense that something was up; the conversations dimmed, and the banjo music stopped. Thank God.

Rita cleared her throat. "Could I get some dried pickled plums?"

"*Umeboshi?*"

"Yeah, those."

"Well, sure, if you like."

Rachel took out a small plate and started piling it with *umeboshi* from a large, plastic bucket.

"I don't need the plate."

"I'm sorry?"

"That thing you're holding in your left hand. Yeah, the bucket. I'll take all of them."

"Um, people don't usually eat that many at once," Rachel said.

"That a problem?"

"No, I suppose not—"

"Thanks for your help."

Bucket in hand, Rita walked back triumphantly. She thunked it down in the middle of the table right in front of me.

The container was about thirty centimeters across at the mouth—

a tub big enough to serve about two hundred men, since nobody ever wanted more than one—packed halfway to the top with bright red *umeboshi*. Big enough to drown a small cat. The base of my tongue started to ache just looking at it. Rita went for her chopsticks.

She singled out one of the wrinkled, reddish fruit from the bucket and popped it into her mouth. She chewed. She swallowed. Out came the pit.

"Not sour at all." Her eyes watered.

Rita passed the barrel to me with a shove. My turn. I picked out the smallest one I could find and put it in my mouth. I ate it and spit out the pit.

"Mine either."

We were playing our own game of gastronomic chicken. The tips of Rita's chopsticks quivered as she plunged them back into the barrel. She tried twice to pick up another *umeboshi* between them before she gave up and just skewered one on a single stick, lifting it to her mouth. The fruit trailed drops of pink liquid that stained the tray where they fell.

A crowd of onlookers had begun to gather around us. They watched in uneasy silence at first, but the excitement grew palpably with each pit spat out on the tray.

Sweat beaded on our skin like condensation on a hot day's beer can. The revolting pile of half-chewed pits grew. Rachel was off to the side, watching with a worried smile. I spotted my friend from the 4th in the throng, too. He was having such a good time watching me suffer. Each time Rita or I put another *ume* in our mouths, a wave of heckling rippled through the crowd.

"Come on, pick up the pace!"

"No turnin' back now, keep 'em poppin'!"

"You're not gonna let this little girl show you up, are you?"

"Fuck, you think he can beat Rita? You're crazy!"

"Eat! Eat! Eat!"

"Watch the doors, don't want nobody breakin' this up! I got ten bucks on the scrawny guy!" followed immediately by, "Twenty on Rita!" Then someone else cried out, "Where's my fried shrimp? I lost my fried shrimp!"

It was hot, it was loud, and in a way I can't explain, it felt like home. There was an invisible bond that hadn't been there my previous times through the loop. I'd had a taste of what tomorrow would bring, and suddenly all the little things that happen in our lives, the minutiae of the day, took on new importance. Just then, being surrounded by all that noise felt good.

In the end, we ate every industrially packed *umeboshi* in the barrel. Rita had the last one. I argued that it was a tie, but since Rita had gone first, she insisted that she had won. When I objected, Rita grinned and offered to settle it over another barrel. It's hard to say whether that grin meant she really could have gone on eating or if the overload of sour food had made her a little funny in the head. The gorilla from the 4th brought in another full barrel of the red fruit from Hell and placed it in the middle of the table with a thud.

By that point, I felt like I was made of *umeboshi* from the waist on down. I waved the white flag.

After that, I talked with Rita about everything—Yonabaru who never shut up, Sergeant Ferrell and his training obsession, the rivalry between our platoon and the 4th. For her part, Rita told me things she hadn't had time to get to in the last loop. When not encased in her Jacket, the Bitch wore a shy smile that suited her well. Her fingertips smelled of machine grease, pickled plum, and a hint of coffee.

I don't know which flags I'd set or how, but on that 160th loop my relationship with Rita deepened as it never had before. The next morning, Corporal Jin Yonabaru didn't wake up on the top bunk. He woke up on the floor.

∃

I found no peace in sleep. A Mimic would snuff out my life, or I'd black out in the middle of battle. After that, nothing. Then without warning, the nothingness gave way. The finger that had been squeezing the trigger of my rifle was wedged three quarters of the way through my paperback. I'd find myself lying in bed, surrounded by its pipe frame, listening to the high-pitched voice of the DJ read the day's weather. *Clear and sunny out here on the islands, same as yesterday, with a UV warning for the afternoon.* Each word wormed its way into my skull and stuck there.

By "sunny" I had picked up the pen, by "islands" I was writing the number on my hand, and by the time she'd gotten to "UV warning" I was out of bed and on my way to the armory. That was my wake-up routine.

Sleep on the night before the battle was an extension of training. For some reason, my body never grew fatigued. The only thing I brought with me were my memories and the skills I'd mastered. I spent the night tossing and turning, my mind replaying the movements it had learned the previous day as it burned the program into my brain. I had to be able to do what I couldn't the last time through the loop, to kill the Mimics I couldn't kill, to save the friends I couldn't save. Like doing an iso push-up in my mind. My own private nightly torment.

I awoke in battle mode. Like a pilot flipping through switches before takeoff, I inspected myself one part at a time, checking for any muscles that might have knotted up overnight. I didn't skip so much as a pinky toe.

Rotating ninety degrees on my ass, I sprang out of bed and

opened my eyes. I blinked. My vision blurred. The room was different. The prime minister's head wasn't staring out at me from atop the swimsuit model. By the time I noticed, it was too late; my foot missed a platform that wasn't there and my inertia sent me tumbling from the bed. My head slammed into a tile-covered floor, and I finally realized where I was.

Sunlight shone through layers of blast-resistant glass and spilled across the vast, airy room. An artificial breeze from the purifier poured over my body as I lay sprawled on the floor. The thick walls and glass completely blocked out the sounds of the base that were usually so loud in my ears.

I was in the Sky Lounge. In a base of exposed steel and khaki-colored, fire-retardant wood, this was the one and only properly appointed room. Originally an officers' meeting room that doubled as a reception hall, the night view of Uchibo through its multi-layered glass would have fetched a good price.

As nice as the view was, it was a lousy place to wake up, unless you were a mountain goat or a dedicated hermit with a love of heights. Or you could be Yonabaru. I'd heard he had some secret spot up here one floor higher than even the officers were allowed to go. "His love nest," we called it.

More like a love aerie.

Looking out across the ocean I could see the gentle curve of the horizon. Uchibo beach was dimly visible through the morning mist. Triangles of waves rose, turned to foam, and faded back into the sea. Beyond those waves lay the island the Mimics had made their spawning grounds. For a moment, I thought I saw a bolt of bright green shoot through the surf. I blinked my eyes. It had only been a glint of sunlight on the water.

"You certainly slept well last night." Rita stood over me, having walked in from the other room.

I looked up slowly from the tile floor. "Feels like it's been years."

"Years?"

"Since I had a good night's sleep. I'd forgotten how good it is."

"That's crazy time-loop talk."

"You should know."

Rita gave a wave of her hand in sympathy.

Our savior, the Full Metal Bitch, looked more relaxed this morning than I had ever seen her. Her eyes were softer in the cool morning light, and the sunlight made her rust-colored hair glow orange. She gave me the sort of look she might give to a puppy who'd followed her home. She was placid as a Zen monk. She was beautiful.

The room suddenly grew too bright, and I narrowed my eyes against the glare. "What's that smell?"

An unusual odor mingled with the clean air coming from the filter. It wasn't necessarily a bad smell, but I wouldn't have gone so far as to call it pleasant. Too pungent for food, too savory for perfume. Quite frankly, I didn't know what the hell it was.

"All I did was open the bag. You've got a sharp nose."

"In training they told us to be wary of any unusual odors, since it could mean there was a problem with the Jacket filter—not that I'm in a Jacket right now."

"I've never met anyone who confused food with chemical weapons before," Rita said. "Don't you like the smell?"

"Like isn't the word I'd use. It smells . . . weird."

"No manners at all. Is that any way to thank me for boiling a morning pot of coffee for us?"

"That's . . . coffee?"

"Sure is."

"This isn't your way of getting back at me for the *umeboshi*, is it?"

"No, this is what roasted coffee beans picked from actual coffee trees that grew in the ground smell like. Never had any?"

"I have a cup of the artificial slop every day."

"Just wait till I brew it. You ain't smelled nothin' yet."

I didn't know there were any natural coffee beans left in the world. That is, I suspected real coffee still existed, somewhere, but I didn't know there was anyone still in the habit of drinking it.

The beverage that passed for coffee these days was made from lab-grown beans with artificial flavoring added for taste and aroma. Substitute grounds didn't smell as strong as the beans Rita was grinding, and they didn't fight their way into your nose and down your entire respiratory tract like these did, either. I suppose you could extrapolate the smell of the artificial stuff and eventually approach the real thing, but the difference in impact was like the difference between a 9mm hand gun and a 120mm tank shell.

"That must be worth a small fortune," I said.

"I told you we were on the line in North Africa before we came here. It was a gift from one of the villages we freed."

"Some gift."

"Being queen isn't all bad, you know."

A hand-cranked coffee grinder sat in the middle of the glass table. A uniquely shaped little device—I'd seen one once in an antique shop. Beside it was some kind of ceramic funnel covered with a brown-stained cloth. I guessed you were supposed to put the ground-up coffee beans in the middle and strain the water through them.

An army-issued portable gas stove and heavy-duty frying pan dominated the center of the table. A clear liquid bubbled noisily in the frying pan. Two mugs sat nearby, one chipped with cracked paint, and one that looked brand new. At the very edge of the table sat a resealable plastic bag filled with dark brown coffee beans.

Rita didn't seem to have many personal effects. There was nothing in the way of luggage save a semi-translucent sack at the foot of the table—it looked like a boxer's heavy bag. Without the coffee-making equipment to support it, the bag had collapsed, nearly empty. Soldiers who had to be ready to ship out to the far corners of the earth at a moment's notice weren't permitted much cargo, but even by those standards Rita traveled light. That one of the few things she did bring was a hand-powered coffee grinder didn't do anything to lessen the perception that she was a little odd.

"You can wait in bed if you like."

"I'd rather watch," I said. "This is interesting."

"Then I guess I'll get grinding."

Rita started turning the handle on the coffee grinder. A gravelly crunching sound filled the room and the glass table shook. Rita's curls quaked atop her head.

"When the war's over, I'm gonna treat you to the best green tea you ever had—in return for the coffee."

"I thought green tea came from China."

"It may have started there, but it was perfected here. It was a long time before they'd even allow it to be exported. I wonder what kind we should have."

"They serve it for free in restaurants?"

"That's right."

"*After* the war . . ." Rita sounded just a little sad.

"Hey, this war will be over someday. No doubt about it. You and I'll see to that."

"You're right. I'm sure you will." Rita took the ground beans and spread them on the cloth covering the funnel. "You have to steam them first."

"Oh yeah?"

"Completely changes the flavor. Something an old friend once taught me. Don't know how it works, but he was right."

She moistened the freshly ground beans with a little not-quite boiling water. Cream-colored bubbles hissed to life where the water touched the grounds. A striking aroma woven of threads bitter, sweet, and sour filled the air surrounding the table.

"Still smell weird?"

"It smells wonderful."

Using a circular motion, Rita carefully poured in the water. Drop by drop, a glistening brown liquid began filling the steel mug waiting beneath.

A thin line of steam had begun to rise from the mug when an earsplitting sound pierced the thick walls and blast-hardened glass of the Sky Lounge. The tile floor shook. Rita and I were on the ground in a heartbeat. Our eyes met.

There was no chandelier tinkle of shattered glass, only a sharp concussive sound, as though someone had thrown a thick telephone book onto the ground. Spiderweb fractures spread through the window glass, a sand-colored javelin sticking from the middle of the web. Deep purple liquid crystal seeped from the cracks and onto the floor below.

Too late, sirens began to blare across the base. Three plumes of smoke rose outside the window. The water off the coast had turned a livid green.

"An—an attack?" My voice was shaking. Probably my body too. In all 159 loops there had never been a surprise attack. The battle was supposed to start *after* we landed on Kotoiushi Island.

A second and third round impacted the window. The entire glass pane bulged inward but somehow held. Cracks crisscrossed the window. Pinpricks of light swam before my eyes.

Rita had gotten to her feet and was calmly returning the frying pan to the top of the portable gas stove. She killed the flame with a practiced hand.

"This glass is really something. You never know if it's all just talk," Rita mused.

"We have to hit back—no, I've got to find the sergeant—wait, our Jackets!"

"You should start by calming down."

"But, what's happening!" I hadn't meant to shout, but couldn't help it. None of this was in the script. I'd been looped so long that the idea of novel events terrified me. That the novel event in question happened to involve Mimic javelins exploding against the windows of the room I was standing in didn't help.

"The Mimics use the loops to win the war. You're not the only one who remembers what's happened in each loop."

"Then this is all because I screwed up the last time?"

"The Mimics must have decided this was the only way they could win. That's all."

"But . . . the base," I said. "How did they even get here?"

"They came inland up the Mississippi to attack Illinois once. They're aquatic creatures. It's not surprising they found a way through a quarantine line created by a bunch of land-dwelling humans." Rita was calm.

"I guess."

"Leave the worrying to the brass. For you and me, this just means we fight here instead of Kotoiushi."

Rita held out her hand. I clasped it and she helped me to my feet. Her fingers were callused at the bases—rub marks from the Jacket contact plates. The palm of the hand she'd been holding the frying pan with was much warmer than my own. I could feel the tight apprehension in my chest begin to ebb.

"A Jacket jockey's job is to kill every Mimic in sight. Right?"

"Yeah. Yeah, that's right."

"We'll go to the U.S. hangar first. I'll put on my Jacket. We'll get weapons for both of us. I'll cover you on our way to the Japanese hangar. Got it?"

"Got it."

"Then we hunt down the server and kill it. End the loop. After that, just need to mop up whatever's left." I stopped shaking. Rita flashed an ironclad grin. "No time for our morning cup o' joe."

"Just gotta finish this before it gets cold," I said, reaching for a cup.

"That an attempt at humor?"

"It was worth a try."

"That would be nice though. Coffee never tastes the same when you reheat it. And if you leave the natural stuff sitting out, after about three days it starts to grow mold. That happened to me once in Africa. I coulda kicked myself."

"Was it good?"

"Very funny."

"If you didn't drink it, how do you know it wasn't?"

"You can drink all the moldy coffee you like. Don't expect me to clean up after you when you get sick. Come on."

Rita moved away from the table, leaving behind the freshly brewed, all-natural coffee. As we started to walk from the room, a small woman who'd been pressed up against the door came tumbling in, feathered headdress and all. Her black hair was braided into a ponytail that flopped behind her bizarre choice of headgear. Everybody's favorite Native American, Shasta Raylle.

"We're under attack! We're under attack!" she shouted, nearly breathless. Her face was streaked with lines of red and white warpaint. I began to wonder if the whole loop thing was just me going crazy for the last few seconds of life in a steaming crater somewhere.

Rita took a step back to appreciate one of the brightest minds MIT had to offer. "Which tribe's attacking?"

"Not a tribe! The *Mimics*!"

"This how you always dress for battle?"

"Is it that bad?" Shasta asked.

"I'm not one to criticize someone's customs or religion, but I'd say you're about two hundred years late to the powwow."

"No, you don't understand!" Shasta said. "They forced me to dress up like this at the party last night! This sort of thing always happens when you're not around."

I suppose everyone has a cross to bear, I thought.

"Shasta, why are you here?" Rita said, with surprising patience.

"I came to tell you your axe isn't in the hangar, it's in the workshop."

"Thanks for the heads-up."

"Be careful out there."

"What are you going to do?"

"I can't fight, so I figured I'd find a nice place to hide—"

"Use my room," Rita said quickly. "The javelins can't make it through the walls or the glass. It's tougher than it looks. You just need to do me one little favor."

"A . . . favor?"

"Don't let anyone in here until either he or I come back." Rita jabbed a thumb in my direction. I don't think Shasta even realized there was anyone standing next to Rita until then. I could almost hear her big eyes blinking from somewhere behind her glasses as she stared at me. I hadn't met Shasta Raylle yet in this loop.

"And you are. . .?"

"Keiji Kiriya. A pleasure."

Rita stepped toward the door. "You're not to let anyone in, no matter who they are or what they say. I don't care if it's the president, tell him to go fuck himself."

"Yes sir!"

"I'm counting on you. Oh, and one other thing—"

"Yes?"

"Thanks for the good luck charm. I'll need it."

Rita and I hurried to the hangar.

4

By the time Rita and I had made the relatively long trip from the Sky Lounge, U.S. Special Forces had established a defensive perimeter with their hangar at its center.

Two minutes for Rita to put on her Jacket. One minute forty-five seconds to run to Shasta's workshop. Six minutes fifteen seconds to put down two Mimics we encountered on the way to the Nippon hangar. In all, twelve minutes and thirty seconds had passed since we left the Sky Lounge.

The base had descended into chaos. Tongues of flame shot into the sky and vehicles lay overturned in the roads. Smoky haze filled the alleyways between the barracks, making it difficult to see. The firecracker popping of small arms fire, useless against Mimics, rang through the air, drowned out by the occasional roar of a rocket launcher. Javelins met attack choppers as they scrambled into the sky, shattering their rotor blades and sending them spiraling toward the ground.

For every person running north to flee the carnage, there was another running south. There was no way of knowing which way was safe. The surprise attack had smashed the chain of command. No one at the top had any better idea of what was going on than anyone at the bottom.

There were hardly any Mimic corpses, and of the ten thousand plus Jackets on the base there was no sign at all. Human bodies were scattered here and there. It didn't take more than a glance at a crushed torso to know they were KIAs.

A dead soldier lay face down on the ground thirty meters in front of my hangar. His torso had been shredded to ground beef, but he was still clutching a magazine with both hands. Beneath a thin layer of dust a smiling, topless blond stared up from its pages. I would know those prodigious breasts anywhere. The guy in the bunk next to mine had been looking at them during all those heart-to-heart talks I'd had with Yonabaru in the barracks. It was Nijou.

"Poor bastard died looking at porn," I said.

"Keiji, you know what we have to do."

"Yeah, I know. There's no going back this time. No matter who dies."

"There's not much time. Come on."

"I'm ready." I thought I was, for that one second. "Fuck! This isn't a battle, it's a massacre."

The hangar door stood open. There were marks where someone had jimmied the lock with something like a crowbar. Rita thrust one of the battle axes into the ground and unlatched the 20mm rifle slung on her back.

"You've got five minutes."

"I only need three."

I ran into the hangar. It was a long narrow building with Jackets lining either side of the passage down the middle. Each building housed enough Jackets for one platoon, twenty-five to a wall. The air inside was heavy and moist. The lights set into the walls flickered off and on. Most of the Jackets still hung from their hooks, lifeless.

The overpowering stench of blood almost knocked me off my feet. A huge dark pool had collected in the center of the room, staining the concrete. Enough to fill a bird bath. Two lines that looked as though they'd been painted with a brush extended from the pool toward the other entrance at the far end of the hangar.

Someone had been horribly wounded here, and whoever dragged them away didn't have the manpower or equipment to do it neatly. If all that blood had leaked out of one person, they were already dead. A handful of Jackets were strewn in disarray on the ground, like the desiccated molts of some human-shaped beast.

A Jacket was a lot like one of those ridiculous cuddly suits employees dress up in at theme parks to look like some maniacally grinning mouse. When they're empty, they just hang on the wall with gaping holes in the back waiting for someone to climb in.

Since Jackets read minute muscular electric signals, each one has to be custom made. If you were to wear someone else's Jacket, there's no telling what would happen. It might not move at all, or it might snap your bones like twigs, but whatever the result, it wouldn't be good. No one made it out of Basic without learning at least that much. The Jackets on the ground were clear evidence that someone had ignored that basic rule out of desperate necessity. I shook my head.

My Jacket had been left unmolested in its berth. I climbed in. Of the thirty-seven pre-suit-up checks, I skipped twenty-six.

A shadow moved at the far end of the hangar where the blood trails led—the end of the hangar Rita wasn't watching. My nervous system jumped into panic mode. I was twenty meters from the door, maybe less. A Mimic could cover the distance in under a second. A javelin even faster.

Could I kill a Mimic with my bare hands? No. Could I deal with it? Yes. Mimics moved faster than even a Jacketed human could, but their movements were easy to read. I could dodge its charge and press tight against the wall to buy enough time to work my way to Rita. Unconsciously, I assumed a battle posture, rotating my right leg clockwise and my left counterclockwise. Then the shadow's identity finally clicked: it was Yonabaru.

He was covered in blood from the waist down. Dried blood caked his forehead. He looked like a sloppy painter. A smile replaced the tension in his face, and he started running toward me.

"Keiji, shit, I haven't seen you all morning. Was startin' to worry."

"That makes two of us. Glad you're all right." I canceled the evasion program my body was running and stepped over the clothes I'd left on the floor.

"Whaddayou think you're doin'?" he asked.

"What's it look like? I'm going to kill some Mimics."

"You crazy? This isn't the time."

"You have something better to do?"

"I dunno, how about a nice orderly retreat, or findin' a place the Mimics aren't and goin' there. Or maybe just runnin' the fuck away!"

"The Americans are suiting up. We need to join them."

"They're not us. Forget 'em. If we don't leave now, we may not get another chance."

"If we run, who'll be left to fight?"

"Have you lost it? Listen to yourself!"

"This is what we trained for."

"The base is lost, dude, it's fucked."

"Not while Rita and I are here it's not."

Yonabaru grabbed my Jacketed arm, actually trying to tug me along like a child pulling with all his weight on his father's hand to get to the toy store. "You're talkin' crazy, dude. There's nothin' you or me can do that'll make a difference," he said with another tug. "Maybe this is your idea of duty, honor, all that shit. But believe me, ain't none of us got a duty to get ourselves killed for nothin'. Me and you are just ordinary soldiers. We're not like Ferrell or those guys in Special Forces. The battle doesn't need us."

"I know." I shook off Yonabaru's hand with the slightest of twitches. "But I need the battle."

"You really mean it, don't you?"

"I don't expect you to understand."

Rita was waiting for me. I'd taken four minutes.

"Don't say I didn't warn ya."

I ignored Yonabaru's glib comment and ran out of the hangar. Rita and I weren't the only soldiers wearing Jackets now. My HUD was sprinkled with icons indicating other friendlies. Clustered in groups of two or three, they'd taken cover in the barracks or behind overturned vehicles where they could spring out at intervals to fire short bursts with their rifles.

The Mimic surprise attack had been flawless. The soldiers were completely cut off from command. Even those wearing Jackets weren't fighting like a disciplined platoon—it was more like an armed mob. For armored infantry to be effective against a Mimic, they had to fan out from cover and throw everything they had at the enemy just to slow them down. One on one, even two on one, they didn't stand a chance.

Friendly icons blinked onto my display, then winked out. The number of friendlies was holding steady solely thanks to U.S. Special Forces. The number of Mimic icons was steadily increasing. Half the comm traffic was static, and the rest was a mix of panicked screams and "Fuck! Fuck! Fuck!" I didn't hear anyone giving orders. Yonabaru's dire predictions didn't look far off.

I opened a comm channel to Rita. "What now?"

"Do what we do best. Kill some Mimics."

"Anything more specific?"

"Follow me. I'll show you."

We joined the battle. Rita's crimson Jacket was a banner for our fragmented army to rally behind. We moved from one lone soldier to the next, herding them together. Until the last Mimic was dead, we'd keep at it.

The Valkyrie flew from one end of Flower Line to the other at will, carrying her unspoken message of hope to all who saw her. Even the Japanese troops, who'd never seen her Jacket in person, much less fought at her side, gained a renewed sense of purpose at the sight of that glittering red steel. Wherever she went, the heart of the battle followed.

In her Jacket, Rita was invincible. Her sidekick, yours truly, might have had an Achilles' heel or two, but I was more than a match for any Mimic. Humanity's enemy had met its executioners. It was time to show the Mimics just how deep into Hell they'd fallen.

Lifting energy packs and ammo from the dead, we kicked and stomped a jitterbug of death across the battlefield. If a building got in our way, we carved a new path through with our battle axes. We detonated a fuel depot to destroy an entire mob of Mimics. We wrenched off part of the antenna tower's base and used it as a barricade. The Full Metal Bitch and the squire at her side were steel death incarnate.

We came across a man hidden behind the burning hulk of an armored car. A Mimic was bearing down on him, and I knew without being told that this one was mine to take care of. I struck, and the Mimic fell. Quickly, I put myself between the Mimic's corpse and the man to protect him from the conductive sand spilling out of its body. Without a Jacket to filter the nanobots, the sand was deadly.

Rita secured a perimeter around the wounded man. Smoke billowed from the car, reducing visibility to next to nothing. Ten meters away, at about six o'clock, lay a steel tower that had fallen on its side. Beyond that, our Doppler was swarming with white points of light. If we stayed here we'd be overrun by Mimics.

The man's leg was pinned beneath the overturned vehicle. He was well-muscled, and an old film camera hung from a neck which was much thicker than my own. It was Murdoch, the journalist who'd been snapping pictures at Rita's side during PT.

Rita kneeled and examined his leg. "I thought you tried to stay *out* of battle."

"It was a good shot, Sergeant Major. A Pulitzer for sure, if I'd managed to take it. Didn't count on the explosion, though." Soot and grime fouled the corners of his mouth.

"I don't know whether that makes you lucky or unlucky."

"Meeting a goddess in Hell must mean I still have some luck," he said.

"This armor plate is dug into your leg pretty deep. It'll take too long to get you out."

"What are my options?"

"You can stay here shooting pictures until the Mimics crush you to death, or I can cut off your leg and carry you to the infirmary. Take your pick."

"Rita, wait!"

"You have one minute to think it over. The Mimics are coming." She rose her axe, not really interested in offering him the full sixty seconds.

Murdoch took a deep breath. "Can I ask you something?"

"What?"

"If I live—will you let me take a proper picture of you? No tongues sticking out, no middle fingers?"

"Deal," the Valkyrie replied. Her axe swung down.

The Japanese and U.S. troops met up just over two hours after the attack had begun. In the time it had taken the sun to climb out of the eastern sky and shine down from directly overhead, the soldiers on the ground had cobbled together something you could actually call a front. It was an ugly battle, but it wasn't a rout. There were plenty of men still alive, still moving, still fighting.

Rita and I ran across the remains of the base.

5

The front ran down the middle of Flower Line Base, cutting a bulging half-circle that faced the shoreline. U.S. Special Forces anchored the center of the ragged arc where the enemy attacks were most fierce. Soldiers piled sandbags, hid among the rubble, and showered the enemy with bullets, rockets, and harsh language when they could.

If you drew an imaginary line from the U.S. soldiers to Kotoiushi Island, the No. 3 Training Field would be smack dab in the middle. That's where the Mimics had come ashore. Generally, Mimics behaved with all the intellect of a piece of gardening equipment. Surprise attacks weren't in their military repertoire. And you could be sure that their weak point—the server calling the shots—would be heavily defended, surrounded by the bulk of the Mimic force. Missiles that dug under and shattered bedrock, cluster bombs that fragmented into a thousand bomblets, vaporized fuel-air bombs that incinerated anything near them. All of mankind's tools of technological destruction were useless on their own. Defeating the Mimics was like defusing a bomb; you had to disarm each piece in the proper order or it would blow up in your face.

Rita's Jacket and mine were a perfect match, blood and sand. One axe covering the other's back. We dodged javelins, sliced through Mimics, blasted holes in concrete with tungsten carbide spikes. All in search of the Mimic whose death could end this.

I knew the routine well enough: destroy the antenna and the backups to prevent the Mimics from sending a signal into the past. I thought I'd gotten it right on my 159th loop, and it wasn't likely Rita had screwed things up. But somehow everything had reset again. Getting to know Rita a little more intimately on this

160th loop had been nice, but in exchange Flower Line had taken it on the chin. There would be heavy noncombat personnel casualties and a lot of dead when the dust had finally settled.

I could tell that Rita had an idea. She'd been through more loops than I had, so maybe she saw something I didn't. I thought I'd turned myself into a veteran, but next to her I was still a greenhorn fresh out of Basic.

We were standing on the No. 3 Training Field, barbed wire barricade overturned to one side, chain link fence trampled flat along the other three. Mimics packed into the area, shoulder to shoulder—as if they had shoulders. Unable to support the massive weight of the Mimics, the concrete had buckled and cracked. The sun had begun to sink lower in the sky, casting complex shadows across the uneven ground. The wind was as strong as it had been the day before, but the Jacket's filter removed all trace of the ocean from its smell.

Then there it was, the Mimic server. Rita and I spotted it at the same time. I don't know how we knew it was the one, but we knew.

"I can't raise my support squad on comm. We won't have any air support."

"Nothing new for me."

"You remember what to do?"

I nodded inside my Jacket.

"Then let's do this."

The field was packed with ten thousand square meters of Mimics waiting for our axes to send them into death's oblivion. We advanced to meet them.

Four stubby legs and a tail. No matter how many times I saw a Mimic, I'd never be able to think of anything but a dead and bloated frog. To look at them, there was no telling the server from its clients, but Rita and I knew the difference.

They ate earth and shat out poison, leaving behind a lifeless wasteland. The alien intelligence that had created them had mastered space travel and learned to send information through time. Now they were taking our world and turning it into a facsimile of their own, every last tree, flower, insect, animal, and human be damned.

This time we had to destroy the server. No more mistakes. If we didn't, this battle might never end. I put all the inertia I dared behind my axe—a clean hit on the antenna. "Got it!"

The attack came from behind.

My body reacted before I had time to think. On the battlefield, I left my conscious mind out of the business of running my body. The cool, impartial calculations of my subliminal operating system were far more precise than I could ever be.

The concrete at my feet split in two, sending gray dust shooting into the air as though the ground had exploded. My right leg rolled to maintain balance. I still couldn't see what was attacking me. There was no time to swing my massive battle axe into play.

My arms and legs moved to keep pace with my shifting center of gravity. Shudders coursed through my nerves, straining to provide the necessary evasive response in time. If my spine had been hardwired to the armor plating on my back, it would have been clattering up a storm.

I thrust with the butt of my axe. Done right, it would pack a punch similar to that of a pile driver. With the possible exception of the front armor plating on a tank, there weren't many things that could withstand a square hit with 370 kilograms of piercing force.

The blow glanced off. *Fuck!*

A shadow moved at the edge of my vision. No time to get out of the way. I held in the breath I'd taken before the jab with the axe. The hit was coming. There. For an instant my body lifted off the ground, then I was rolling, my vision alternating between sky and ground, sky and ground. I came out of the roll and regained my feet in a single, fluid motion. My axe was at the ready.

There, with one leg still lifted in the air, stood a gunmetal red Jacket. *Rita!*

Maybe she had knocked me out of the way of an attack I hadn't seen coming, or maybe I'd gotten in her way. But she had definitely been the one who sent me careening across the ground.

What the hell. . .?

The red Jacket crouched and charged. The axe blade was a gleaming razor's edge. I surrendered my body to the battle. One hundred fifty-nine loops had trained it to move with ease, and it did. The first strike came from the side, missing me by a hair's breadth. I deflected the second, a vicious overhand swing, with the haft of my axe. Before the third swing could come, I leapt out of harm's way and put some distance between us.

I caught my breath and the reality of the situation sank in.

"What the fuck are you doing?"

Rita walked slowly toward me, battle axe swinging low, almost brushing the ground. She stopped, and her voice crackled over the comm link. Her high, delicate voice, so out of place on the battlefield:

"What's it look like I'm doing?"

"It looks like you're trying to fucking kill me!"

"Humans perceive Mimic transmissions as dreams. Our brains are the antennas that receive those transmissions. But it's not just one-way. Our brains adapt—we become the antennas. I'm not even looping anymore, but I'm still connected; I can still sense the server Mimic because I am still an antenna myself. The migraines are a side effect. You've had them, haven't you?"

"What are you talking about?"

"That's why the loop repeated last time, even though you destroyed the backups. You didn't destroy the antenna—that was me."

"Rita, I don't understand."

"It works both ways. If you become an antenna, the Mimics will still be able to loop. I'm an antenna. You're trapped in a loop. You kill me, the loop doesn't propagate. I kill you, it's for real. Forever. Only one of us can escape."

None of it made any sense. I'd been a new recruit trapped in a time loop I didn't understand. I'd prayed to become as strong as the Valkyrie I saw striding the battlefield. I'd gotten myself turned into a corpse countless times trying to follow in her footsteps, and after 160 tries, I'd finally earned the right to stand at her side. We'd fought together, laughed together, eaten lunch and talked bullshit together. I'd dragged myself through Hell to get near her, and now the world was going to tear us apart. It didn't get much more fucked up than that. The same loop that had made me into the warrior I had become was going to kill me.

"If humanity is going to win, we need someone who can break the loop." Rita's voice was cool and level.

"Wait, there has to be—"

"Now we find out whether that someone is Rita Vrataski or Keiji Kiriya."

Rita charged.

I threw down my rifle; the time needed to take aim and squeeze the trigger was time I didn't have against the Full Metal Bitch. I gripped my battle axe with both hands.

Our fight unfolded across the entire base. We moved from the No. 3 Training Field to the field we'd used for PT, trampling the remains of the tent the general had used to take shelter from the scorching midday sun. We passed the smoldering remains of the 17th Company barracks and crossed axes in front of the hangar. Our blades slid past each other. I ducked to avoid the strike and kept running.

The other soldiers stopped and stared as we passed. Their helmets hid their expressions, but not their shock. And why not? I couldn't believe this was happening either. My mind was in denial, but my body continued to function, oblivious, like the well-oiled machine it had become. With movements honed to perfection, I pressed the attack.

As we approached the U.S. troop line, a green light on my HUD winked on—incoming comm for Rita. The link between our Jackets relayed the transmission to me.

"Chief Breeder to Calamity Dog." A man's voice. Rita slowed almost imperceptibly. I took the opportunity to widen the space between us. The voice continued, "Enemy suppression near ops successful. You look a little busy, need a hand?"

"Negative."

"Any orders?"

"Keep the Japanese out of this. I won't be responsible for what happens if they get in my way."

"Copy that. Good hunting. Chief Breeder out."

The channel closed, and I screamed at Rita. "That all you got to say? Hello? What the fuck!" There was no reply. Rita's red Jacket closed on me. No more time to talk. I was too busy fighting for my life.

I didn't know whether Rita was really trying to kill me or only testing me. I was a precision fighting machine without processing cycles to spare on extraneous information. Rita and anything more complicated than *run/parry/dodge* would have to wait. Whatever her intentions, her attacks were deadly real.

The base's main gate was to my right. We were on the path I'd taken all those times to sneak into the U.S. side of the base to steal one of Rita's axes. The line U.S. Special Forces held extended right across the spot where the two beefy sentries had stood.

Rita swung her weapon with no regard for who or what it might hit. I didn't see any reason to bring anyone else into this, so I started backing us away from the line. Cafeteria No. 2 was about one hundred meters ahead. The javelins had taken their toll on the structure, but against all odds, it was still standing. It was a good distance from the line—it would do. A heartbeat later I'd covered the hundred meters and was making my way inside through the door on the far side of the building.

It was a dim twilight inside, just light enough to see. Tables lay on their side, piled into a makeshift barricade in front of the entrance opposite the door I'd come through. Food and half-empty soy sauce bottles lay scattered on the concrete floor. There was no sign of anyone—dead or alive—in the entire room.

This was where I'd spent countless lunches watching Rita eat. Where I'd fought that overgrown ape from 4th Company and played culinary chicken with Rita and a tub full of *umeboshi*. What better place for Rita and me to decide our lives in a duel to the death?

Orange light shone through a hole in the west wall. When I glanced at the chronometer beside my display I could hardly believe eight hours had elapsed since the battle started. It was already dusk. No wonder I felt like my Jacket was lined with lead. I didn't have the muscle for this. My batteries were drained and systems were about to start shutting down. I'd never been in a battle half this long.

Rita's red Jacket crept into the cafeteria. I blocked a horizontal swing with my axe; my Jacket's frame creaked. If I'd stopped it head on, the torque from the actuators would have torn my Jacket apart from the inside out. Fear of what Rita was capable of gripped me anew. Rita Vrataski was a prodigy in battle—and she had learned to read my every parry and feint.

Each move in battle happens at a subconscious level. This makes it doubly difficult to compensate when someone learns to read those moves. Rita was half a step ahead of me, already spinning to deliver a deadly blow to the space where I would be before I even got there.

It hit home. I instinctively stepped into the arc of her axe, narrowly avoiding the full brunt of the swing. My left shoulder plate went flying. A red warning light lit up on my display.

Rita kicked, and there was no way to avoid it. I sailed across the room. Sparks flew as my Jacket grated along the broken concrete floor. I spun once and crashed into the counter. A shower of chopsticks rained down on my head.

Rita was already moving. No time to rest. Head, check. Neck, check. Torso, right shoulder, right arm unit—everything but my left shoulder plate checked out. I could still fight. I let go of my axe. Digging my gloves into the counter's edge, I vaulted up and over. Rita swung, shattering the counter and kicking up a spray of wood and metal.

I was in the kitchen. Before me stretched an enormous stainless steel sink and an industrial strength gas range. Frying pans and pots large enough to boil entire pigs hung along one wall. Piles of plastic cutlery reached to the ceiling. Neat rows of trays still held uneaten breakfasts, now long cold.

I backed up, knocking platters to the ground in an avalanche of food and molded plastic. Rita was still coming. I threw a pot at her and scored a direct hit. It sounded like a gong as it bounced off her cherry-red Jacket helmet. Apparently not enough to dissuade her. Maybe I should have tried the kitchen sink instead. With a swing of her axe, Rita destroyed half the counter and a steel-reinforced concrete pillar.

I backed up further—into a wall. I dropped to the ground as a vicious horizontal swing sliced toward me. The bodybuilder's face, still grinning mindlessly down over the kitchen, took the hit in my place. I dove for Rita's legs. She sprang out of the way. I let the momentum carry me back to the ruins of the cafeteria counter. My axe was right where I'd left it.

Picking up a weapon you'd already thrown away could only mean one thing: you were ready to fight back; no one picked up a weapon they didn't plan on using. It was clear I couldn't keep running forever. If Rita really wanted to kill me—and I was starting to think she just might—there would be no running. Fending off one attack after another had left my Jacket running on empty. It was time to make up my mind.

There was one thing I couldn't let myself forget. Something I'd promised myself a long time ago when I resolved to fight my way out of this loop. Hidden beneath the gauntlet on my left hand was the number 160. Back when that number was only 5, I had made a decision to take all I could learn with me into the next day. I'd never shared the secret of those numbers with anyone. Not Rita, not Yonabaru, not even Ferrell who I'd trained with so many times. Only I knew what it meant.

That number was my closest friend, and so long as it was there, I had no fear of dying. It didn't matter if Rita killed me. I would never have made it this far without her anyway. What could be more fitting than redeeming my savior with my own death?

But if I gave up now, everything would be gone. The guts I'd spilled on that crater-blasted island. The blood I'd choked on. The arm I'd left lying on the ground. The whole fucking loop. It would vanish like the smoke out of a gun barrel. The 159 battles that didn't exist anywhere but in my head would be gone forever, meaningless.

If I gave it all I had and lost, that was one thing. But I wasn't going to die without a fight. Rita and I were probably thinking the same thing. I understood what she was going through. Hell, she and I were the only two people on the whole damn planet who could understand. I'd crawled over every inch of Kotoiushi Island trying to find a way to survive, just as Rita had done on some battlefield back in America.

If I lived, she'd die, and I'd never find someone like her again. If she lived, I would have to die. No matter how many different ways I ran it through my head, there didn't seem to be another way out. One of us had to die, and Rita didn't want to talk it through. She was going to let our skill decide. She'd chosen to speak with steel, and I had to give her an answer.

I picked up my axe.

I ran to the middle of the cafeteria and tested its weight. I found myself standing almost exactly where Rita and I had gone through the *umeboshi*. Ain't life funny? It was only a day ago, but it felt like a lifetime. Rita had beaten me at that, too. I think it was fair to say she had a gift for competition.

Rita's crimson Jacket advanced one step at a time, sizing me up. She stopped just outside of axe range, her gleaming weapon gripped tightly in her hand.

The sounds of the fighting outside intruded on the quiet of the cafeteria. Explosions were the beat of distant drums. Shells tearing through the sky were the high notes of flutes. Automatic rifles played a staccato percussion. Rita and I brought together raucous cymbals of tungsten carbide.

There were no cheering onlookers in the crumbling ruins of the cafeteria. Piles of tables and overturned chairs were our only spectators, silent observers to the deadly dance of our crimson and sand Jackets. We moved in a spiral, as Rita always did, tracing a pattern in the concrete floor. We were dancing a war ballet, wrapped in the pinnacle of mankind's technology, our crude weapons singing a thousand-year-old dirge.

My axe blade was notched and dull. My Jacket was covered in scars, its battery all but depleted. My muscles moved by sheer willpower alone.

A tremendous explosion shook the cafeteria. We jumped at the sound.

I knew her next strike would be a killing blow. There would be no avoiding it. No time to think—thinking was for training. Battle was all about action. The experience etched into my body through 159 battles would guide my movements.

Rita pulled her axe back for the swing. My axe would answer from below. The two giant blades crossed, shredding plates of armor.

There was only one real difference between Rita and me. Rita had learned to fight the Mimics alone. I had learned to fight the Mimics watching Rita. The precise moment she would swing, the next step she would take—my operating system had recorded it all. I knew what her next move would be. That's why Rita's swing only grazed me, and my swing tore open her Jacket.

A hole gaped in Rita's crimson armor.

"Rita!"

Her battle axe trembled in her hands. Rita's Jacket was doing its best to filter the unintended commands triggered by the convulsions in her muscles. The axe's tungsten carbide handle clattered noisily against her gauntlets. Blood, oil, and some unidentifiable fluids oozed from the newly opened split in her armor. The scene was eerily familiar to me, and I felt a renewed sense of terror. She extended her arm and fumbled for the jack on my shoulder plate. A contact comm. Rita's voice was clear in my helmet.

"You win, Keiji Kiriya." The crimson Jacket leaned hard against me. Rita's voice was dry and laced with pain.

"Rita—why?"

"I've known for a long time. Ever since I first got the Mimic signal. The battle always ends."

"What? I don't—"

"You're the one who makes it out of this loop." Rita coughed, a mechanical sputtering sound through the link.

I finally understood. When I met Rita yesterday, she had decided that she was going to die. I didn't recognize it for what it was at the time. I thought I'd accidentally tripped some sort of flag. I should have been trying to find a way to save her, but I let the day slip through my fingers.

"I'm sorry, Rita. I—I didn't know."

"Don't apologize. You won."

"Won? Can't we just . . . just keep repeating this? We may never leave the loop, but we'll be together. Forever. We can be together longer than a lifetime. Every day will be a battle, but we can handle battle. If I have to kill a thousand Mimics, a million, I will. We'll do it together."

"Every morning you'll wake up to a Rita Vrataski who doesn't know you exist."

"I don't care."

Rita shook her head. "You don't have a choice. You have to break out of the loop before what happened to me happens to you. End this goddamn thing while you still can."

"I can't sacrifice you to do it."

"The Keiji Kiriya I know wouldn't sacrifice the human race for himself."

"Rita—"

"There isn't much time. If there's something you want to say, say it now." The crimson Jacket slumped.

"I'll stay with you until you die. I—I love you."

"Good. I don't want to die alone."

Her face was hidden beneath her helmet, and I was grateful. If I'd been able to see her tears, I never could have ended the loop and left her forever. Light from the setting sun, red and low in the western sky, played across Rita's crimson Jacket, enveloping her in a brilliant ruby glow.

"Long fight, Keiji. It's already sunset."

"It's beautiful."

"Sentimental bastard." There was a smile in her voice. "I hate red skies."

It was the last thing she ever said.

6

The sky was bright.

Rita Vrataski was dead. After I killed the Mimic server and mopped up the stragglers, they threw me in the brig. They said it was for dereliction of duty. By recklessly ignoring the orders of a superior officer, I had placed my fellow soldiers in harm's way. Never mind that there hadn't been any superior officers to give any fucking orders. They were scrambling to find someone to pin Rita's death on, and I couldn't blame them for wanting a scapegoat.

The court martial took place three days after they locked me up; I was cleared of the charges. In the end, they decided to pin a medal on me instead.

A general, the one who had ordered up the PT, patted me on the back and told me what a fine job I'd done. He all but rolled his eyes when he said it. I wanted to tell him to shove the medal up his ass for all the good it would do, but I stopped myself. Rita's death was my responsibility. No point in taking it out on him.

The medal was the Order of the Valkyrie, awarded to soldiers who killed over one hundred Mimics in a single battle. An award originally created for one very special soldier. The only way to receive a higher honor was to die in battle—like Rita had.

I really had killed a lot of the fuckers. More than all of Rita's kills combined in just one battle. I don't remember much of what happened after I destroyed the server, but apparently I found a replacement battery for my suit and proceeded to single-handedly take out somewhere around half of all the Mimics that had attacked Flower Line.

Reconstruction of the base had been moving forward at a fever pitch. Half the buildings on the base had burned to the ground, and hauling off the wreckage was a monumental task in and of itself. The 17th Company's barracks were gone, and the mystery novel I'd never gotten around to finishing was nothing but ashes.

I wandered aimlessly as people hurried to and fro across the base.

"Fight like a motherfuckin' maniac? That how decorated heroes do?"

The voice was familiar. I turned just in time to see a fist flying straight at me. My left leg repositioned itself. I didn't have time to think. All I could do was decide whether or not to throw the counterattack switch in my head. If I flipped the switch on, the reflexes burned into me through 160 loops would kick in, taking over my body like a robot in a factory.

I could shift my weight to my left leg, deflect the punch with my shoulder, and grab my attacker's elbow as I stepped forward with my right foot and jammed my own elbow into his side. That would take care of the first punch. I ran the simulation in my head and realized I'd be shattering my assailant's ribs before I even knew who he was. I opted to just take the punch. The worst I would walk away with was a black eye.

It hurt more than I'd bargained for. The force of the blow knocked me back, and I landed hard on my ass. At least nothing was broken— all according to plan. It was good to know I had a career of being a punching bag ahead of me if the army didn't pan out.

"I don't know about you bein' a prodigy, but you sure as fuck are full of yourself."

"Leave him alone."

Yonabaru was standing over me. He looked like he wanted to keep throwing punches, but a woman in a plain soldier's shirt had stepped in to stop him. Her left arm was in a sling. The bleached white cloth stood in sharp contrast to her khaki shirt. She must have been Yonabaru's girlfriend. I was glad they'd both survived.

There was a light in the woman's eyes unlike any I'd ever seen before, as though she were watching a lion that had broken free of its chains. It was a look reserved for something other than human.

"Come strollin' in here like nothin' happened—makes me sick just lookin' at you."

"I said, leave him alone."

"Fuck him."

Before I could stand up, Yonabaru had walked off. I stood slowly and dusted myself off. My jaw didn't hurt too badly. It was nothing compared to the emptiness Rita had left inside me.

"He landed a good one," I heard from behind me. It was Ferrell. He looked the same as always, with maybe another wrinkle or two in his forehead to show for the fight.

"You saw that?"

"Sorry, I didn't have time to stop him."

"It's okay."

"Try not to hold it against him. He lost a lot of friends that day. He just needs some time to settle down."

"I saw Nijou—what was left of him."

"Our platoon lost seventeen men. They're saying three thousand casualties all together, but there's no official number yet. You remember that pretty young lady who ran Cafeteria No. 2? She didn't make it, either."

"Oh."

"It's not your fault, but that hardly matters at a time like this. You know, you gave Yonabaru's lady friend quite a kick. Among others."

"Others?"

"Others."

Add Ferrell to the list of people I'd walked all over in the battle. Who knew what else I'd done. I couldn't remember a damn thing, but it was clear I had been a homicidal maniac on the battlefield. Maybe I was the one who'd put Yonabaru's girlfriend's arm in that sling. No wonder he was so pissed. A kick from a Jacket would be more than enough to do that. Hell, you could liquefy internal organs with ease.

I hoped Yonabaru would remember that fear. It would help keep him alive in the next battle. He may not have thought of me as a friend anymore, but he was still a friend to me.

"I'm sorry."

"Forget it." Ferrell definitely wasn't angry. If anything, he seemed grateful. "Who taught you to pilot a Jacket like that?"

"You did, Sergeant."

"I'm serious, son. If we were talkin' formation drills that would be one thing, but there's not a soldier in the entire Japanese Corps who could teach you to fight like that."

Sergeant Bartolome Ferrell had more battles under his belt than almost anyone in the UDF. He knew what a warrior was. He understood that if I hadn't kicked him out of the way, he'd be dead. He knew that the green recruit standing in front of him was a better warrior than he could ever hope to become. And he knew that in battle, the only rank that mattered was how good you were.

Sergeant Ferrell was responsible for the foundation I'd built my skills on. But I couldn't begin to explain it to him, so I didn't try.

"Oh, almost forgot. Some mouse of a woman from the U.S. Corps been askin' for you."

Shasta Raylle. A Shasta Raylle I'd only met briefly in the Sky Lounge. We'd hardly spoken at all. The Shasta I'd borrowed a battle axe from was a figment of the loop now.

"Where are the 17th's temp barracks? And what about the hangar? I'd like to check on my Jacket."

"Just out of the brig and you want to check your Jacket? You're the real deal."

"I'm nothing special."

"The U.S. squad took your Jacket. Come to think of it, that mouse was one of the ones who came to take it."

"What do they want with my Jacket?"

"The brass has plans. Don't be surprised if you wind up in U.S. Special Forces."

"Seriously?"

"They need someone to take the Valkyrie's place. I'm sure you'll fit right in." Ferrell clapped me on the shoulder and we parted ways.

I headed for the American side of the base to find Shasta and my Jacket. The barracks and roads were so badly burnt it was hard to tell where the Japanese side ended and the U.S. side began. Even the sentries and all their muscles were gone.

I found my Jacket in Shasta's workshop. Shasta was there too. Someone had scratched the words "Killer Cage" into the breast-plate. "Cage"—that was how the Americans pronounced my name. I guess I had a call sign of my own now. They didn't waste much time. It was a good name for a pig's ass who won medals by kill-ing his friends. I'd have to thank whoever thought of it. What a fucked-up world.

Shasta saw me staring at the inscription. "I kept as close an eye on it as I could, but they got to it anyway. Sorry." I had the feeling she'd said something similar to Rita in the past.

"Don't worry about it. They told me you were looking for me?"

"I wanted to give you the key to the Sky Lounge."

"Key?"

"Like Rita asked me to. No one's been inside since you left. It wasn't easy keeping people out for three whole days, but I can be very resourceful." Shasta handed me a key card. "Just ignore the stuff by the entrance."

"Thanks."

"Glad I could help."

"Can I ask you something?"

"What?"

"Do you—do you know why Rita painted her Jacket red? It was hardly her favorite color. I thought you might know."

"She said she wanted to stand out. I'm not sure why anyone would want to stand out on a battlefield. Just makes for an easier target."

"Thanks. That makes sense."

"I suppose you'll want horns on yours?" I must have frowned because she immediately added, "Sorry! I was only joking."

"It's fine. I need to learn to watch that scowl. Thanks again for the key. I'm gonna go check out that Sky Lounge."

"Before you go—"

"Yeah?"

"It's none of my business, but I was wondering . . ."

"What is it?" I asked.

"Were you an old friend of Rita's?"

I pressed my lips together into a wry smile.

"I'm sorry, I shouldn't have asked."

"No, it's okay. Actually, we—"

"Yes?"

"We'd only just met."

"Of course. We'd only just come to the base. It was a stupid thing to ask."

I left Shasta and made my way to the Sky Lounge. I opened the door gently, even though I knew I wouldn't be disturbing anyone.

Yellow tape with the word "BIOHAZARD" printed at regular intervals crisscrossed the entryway. There was a fire extinguisher near my feet, and a grainy residue covered the floor. I guessed this was Shasta being resourceful. The base was still covered in conductive sand from the Mimics, and decontaminating non-vital facilities like the Sky Lounge wouldn't rate high on the priority list. Clever.

I stepped inside. The air was stale. Rita's smell was already fading from the room. Nothing had been moved from where we'd left it. The collapsed vinyl bag, coffee grinder, and portable range underscored just how short her stay here had been. They were the only traces she'd even been here. Almost everything else she owned was military-issue. The coffee set was the only personal belongings she had. Of course she hadn't left me a note—that would have been too sentimental for the Full Metal Bitch.

The mug on the glass table still held the coffee Rita had made. I picked up the mug. The coffee was dark and still. It had cooled to room temperature days ago. My hands shook, sending tiny ripples across the jet black surface. This was how Rita had faced her solitude. Now I understood.

You were just a piece on the board, and I was the piece that replaced you. Nothing more than the false hero the world needed. And now this good-for-nothing world was going to push me across the same bloodstained, smoke-filled battlefield. But you never hated the world for what it did to you.

So I wouldn't let the world lose. It could drop me into a field of Mimics with nothing but a tungsten carbide axe and a dying Jacket and I'd fight my way out. I'd march waist-deep in blood through more massacres than all the vets in the UDF had seen combined, and I'd emerge unscathed. I'd train until I knew the precise nanosecond to pull the trigger, the exact moment to take every step. I wouldn't let a javelin so much as scratch the paint on my Jacket.

While I live and breathe, humanity will never fall. I promise you. It may take a dozen years, but I will win this war for you. Even if you won't be here to see it. You were the only person I wanted to protect, and you were gone.

Hot tears threatened to fall from my eyes as I looked out through the cracked glass at the sky, but I wouldn't cry. Not for the friends I would lose in the battles ahead. The friends I wouldn't be able to save. *I won't cry for you until the war is finally over.*

Through the warped window I saw the sky, crystal blue, seeming to stretch forever. A cloud drifted lazily along. I turned to face the window, and like a bone-dry sponge soaking up water, my body absorbed the clear boundless sky.

You hated being alone, but you kept your distance from the barracks, slept and woke in solitude, because it was too hard to face the friends you knew were going to die. Trapped in a cruel, unending nightmare, your only thoughts were for them. You couldn't bear to lose even one of them, no matter who.

Red was your color, yours and yours alone. It should rest with you. I will paint my Jacket sky blue, the color you told me you loved when we first met. In a field of a million soldiers, I will stand out from all the rest, a lightning rod for the enemy's attacks. I will be their target.

I sat there for some time holding the last cup of coffee she'd ever made, for someone she'd barely known. Its thin aroma stirred in me an insufferable longing and sadness. A small colony of blue-green mold bobbed on the surface of the coffee. Raising the cup to my lips, I drank.

Afterword

I like video games. I've been playing them since I was a snot-nosed kid. I've watched them grow up along with me. But even after beating dozens of games on the hardest difficulty mode, I've never been moved to cheer until the walls shake. I've never laughed, cried, or jumped up to strike a victory pose. My excitement drifts like ice on a quiet pond, whirling around somewhere deep inside me.

Maybe that's just the reaction I have watching myself from the outside. I look down from above and say, "After all the time I put into the game, of course I was going to beat it." I see myself with a shit-eating grin plastered on my face—a veteran smile only someone who'd been there themselves could appreciate.

The ending never changes. The village elder can't come up with anything better than the same, worn-out line he always uses. "Well done, XXXX. I never doubted that the blood of a hero flowed in your veins." Well the joke is on you, gramps. There's not a drop of hero's blood in my whole body, so spare me the praise. I'm just an ordinary guy, and proud of it. I'm here because I put in the time. I have the blisters on my fingers to prove it. It had nothing to do with coincidence, luck, or the activation of my Wonder Twin powers. I reset the game hundreds of times until my special attack finally went off perfectly. Victory was inevitable. So please, hold off on all the hero talk.

This is the sort of thing that went through my head while I was writing. Without the help of a great many people, this novel would never have made it into this world. It's a dark story, with characters dying left and right, but I'm happy with how it turned out.

I'd like to thank Yoshitoshi Abe for so perfectly realizing the world of the novel in his illustrations; my chief editor, Miyuki Matsumoto, who went above and beyond the call of duty for the book; After Glow's Takeshi Yamazaki for his wonderful design work; Jun Masuda and his incredible friends for their help checking all things military; and finally Chōhei Kambayashi for his many insightful suggestions.

Oh, I nearly forgot. Thanks to all the good little boys and girls out there sending me those jet-black feeds.

—Hiroshi Sakurazaka

About The Author

Hiroshi Sakurazaka was born in Tokyo in 1970. After a career in information technology, he published his first novel, *Modern Magic Made Simple* (*Yoku wakaru gendai mahou*), in 2003 with Super Dash Bunko, a popular young adult light novel imprint. There are now seven volumes in the series, and it was adapted as a manga in 2008 and as a television anime series in 2009.

Sakurazaka published *All You Need Is Kill* with Super Dash Bunko in 2004 and with it earned his first Seiun Award nomination for best of the year honors in Japanese science fiction. His 2004 short story "Saitama Chainsaw Massacre" won the 16th *SF Magazine* Reader's Award.

In 2009, *All You Need Is Kill* was the launch title for Haikasoru, a unique imprint dedicated to publishing the most compelling contemporary Japanese science fiction and fantasy for English-speaking audiences. *New York Times* best-selling author John Scalzi declared *All You Need Is Kill* to be a novel that "reads fast, kicks ass, and keeps on coming," and it has proven to be one of Haikasoru's most popular titles. Sakurazaka's other novels include *Characters* (cowritten with Hiroki Azuma) and *Slum Online,* which was published in English by Haikasoru in 2010.

In 2010, Sakurazaka started an experimental digital magazine, *AiR,* with Junji Hotta. He remains one of Japan's most energetic writers of both light novels and adult science fiction.

HAIKASORU
THE FUTURE IS JAPANESE

MILITARY SCIENCE FICTION FROM HAIKASORU

YUKIKAZE
–CHŌHEI KAMBAYASHI

In the midst of a war with an enigmatic alien host—a war with no end in sight—Second Lieutenant Rei Fukai carries out his missions in the skies over the strange planet nicknamed "Faery." Attached to Tactical Combat and Surveillance Unit 3 of the Special Air Force, his duty is to gather information on the enemy and bring it back—no matter the cost. His only constant companion in this lonely task is his fighter plane, the sentient FFR-31 Super Sylph, call sign: YUKIKAZE.

GOOD LUCK, YUKIKAZE
–CHŌHEI KAMBAYASHI

The alien JAM have been at war with humanity for over thirty years...or have they? Rei Fukai of the FAF's Special Air Force and his intelligent plane Yukikaze have seen endless battles, but after declaring "Humans are unnecessary now," and forcibly ejecting Fukai, Yukikaze is on her own. Is the target of the JAM's hostility really Earth's machines? And have the artificial intelligences of Earth been acting in concert with the JAM to manipulate Yukikaze? As Rei tries to ascertain the truth behind the intentions of both sides, he realizes that his own humanity may be at risk, and that the JAM are about to make themselves known to the world at large.

GENOCIDAL ORGAN
–PROJECT ITOH

The war on terror exploded, literally, the day Sarajevo was destroyed by a homemade nuclear device. The leading democracies transformed into total surveillance states, and the developing world has drowned under a wave of genocides. The mysterious American John Paul seems to be behind the collapse of the world system, and it's up to intelligence agent Clavis Shepherd to track John Paul across the wreckage of civilizations and to find the true heart of darkness—a genocidal organ.

ALSO BY HIROSHI SAKURAZAKA
SLUM ONLINE

Etsuro Sakagami is a college freshman who simply drifts through life, but when he logs on to the combat MMO Versus Town, he becomes Tetsuo, a karate champ on his way to becoming the most powerful martial artist around. While his relationship with new classmate Fumiko goes nowhere, Etsuro spends his days and nights online in search of the invincible Ganker Jack. Drifting between the virtual and the real, will Etsuro ever be ready to face his most formidable opponent?

VISIT US AT WWW.HAIKASORU.COM